Twisted 2

Billie Dureya Shell

TWISTED 2

Copyright © 2020

All rights reserved to Billie Dureyea Shell.

Front Cover Image By grafic designer Billie Dureyea Shell & Kenny Writes

First Printing Edition 2020

ISBN 9781735023427

Dedication

This book is dedicated to:

My Oldest daughter Jazmine and grandson Jorden

I love you both this one is 4 you

I miss you Nookie...........

Acknowledgement

2020 has been a good year 4 me and my family And that's all becuz our father above so once again I want 2 give thank 2 God for this gift I am so grateful for him giving me away 2 provide 4 my family in my house we will alwayz put you first.

To my mother Mclessie Shell you taught me so much and you loved me NO MATTER WHAT I love you so much momma....
What's up with some bake chicken☐ LOL😁😁☐.

To my little sister Glenda I love you and miss you blackie get at ur big brother Lil Sis.

To my Wife Shatoya Shell you get on my damn nerves☐♂ but I wouldnt trade you 4 anything In the world I Iove♥ you more then words can ever express.

To all my children☐☐☐☐ I love y'all Jazmine, Ant'Tuan, Davon, Anthony, David, Lil Dureyea, Alura, Queen Diavion, Cameron, Preniece, Shaniece and Tajh I love u all and I'll 4ever have ur back you all give me a reason 2 smile...

To my cousin Zane RIP nigga I miss u more then anyone will ever no, your always remembered love you bro. to my cousin

Ty I miss you thank 4 looking out 4 me and Zane you played a big part in my life and

I always looked up to you l love you... Uncle Woody I miss you and love you, you no your my favorite uncle.... To my nigga Jamal love you, my brothers Lawrence and fred thank 4 showing me the game I love yall 4 that. To my oldest sister Nedra love you thank you 4 always having my back. to my family uncles anties cousins etc.. I love y'all even those of you that act funny as fuck

To my dark side niggas y'all no what it is YAAH
GANG........

Now to all my readers and fans I love you thanks for
reading I hope u enjoy this book as much as I enjoy
writing them with this Corona Virus 19 shit there ain't
shit to do but write so I'm on my shit with that being said
y'all be safe cover your face and love each other life is
short so love the ones that really love you

I'm gone enjoy the book

AND STAY SAFE

Author

Billie Dureyea Shell

THERE'S NOTHING U CANNOT DO IF U PUT
UR MIND 2 IT.......

Team Shell

Recap from Book One

After a long day, King wanted to do nothing more than go home and climb into bed. He decided to fix himself a sandwich and watch a little ESPN while he ate. After eating, King stripped down to his boxers and jumped into bed, pulling the covers fully over his head. He would deal with everything going on tomorrow; right now, he just needed a good night of sleep. The sudden feel of heavy pressure on his chest awoke King up from his sleep. His eyes popped wide open at the sight of his wife, straddled across his body, holding a gun to the middle of his forehand. "Baby wait," King screamed. He tried not to make any sudden moves to startle his wife and cause her to accidently pull the trigger on the gun she was holding to the middle of his forehead. "I trusted you," Mya sobbed, lightly brushing the tip of the gun against King's face. King could see the hurt, anger, and betrayal in his wife's eyes. Looking back, King wished he would have just been honest and upfront with his wife months ago. Mya laughed, "Imagine my surprise when I got home this morning to find this in the mailbox," she said, while hitting King across the face with a stack of pictures. King looked down when a few of the photos fell from Mya's hand, and landed on the bed. His mouth opened in shock, That devious bitch, he thought. In the photos, King's head was thrown back in pleasure, which explains how he didn't see the tramp taking the pictures. She had planned this all along. How had he let that sneaky bitch manipulate him into hurting the only woman he truly loved. Mya was his soulmate, his gift from God. "Mya, I love you baby," he gently said. Mya sat quietly as she looked down and stared into her husband's eyes. How had they gotten to this point? Just one year ago, they were saying "I Do" in front of their family and friends during a gorgeous wedding ceremony. The man she gave her virginity too, the man she vowed to love for better or for worse. King and Mya were supposed to be on a flight headed to Hawaii in just a few hours to celebrate their one-year anniversary. But that would never happen now. There would be no celebrations this year, or any other year for that matter. "If you really loved me, you wouldn't have put your dick in that nasty bitch," she screamed, just before pulling the trigger on the gun, filling the room with nothing but silence.

Chapter 1

KING AND MYA

King and Mya stared at each other in silence as feathers from the pillow Mya shot a hole through softly fluttered around the room. King shook his head a few times, trying to stop the loud ringing in his ears. "You're lucky I don't want to put Ms. Brenda through the pain of burying her only child," Mya said, as she threw the gun on the bed and walked over to the closet. Over the past year Mya had grown to love King's mother, Ms. Brenda as her own. King was his mother's sole provider and Mya knew she needed him. That was the only thing that stopped Mya from putting a bullet through the middle of King's forehead. King sat quietly on the bed as Mya grabbed her luggage from the top shelf of the closet and began throwing her clothes inside. King knew he had fucked up and anything he said at that moment would only make their situation worse. He built his empire on the gritty streets of Detroit by having discipline and now wondered how he let himself be tricked into fucking his wife's best friend, Star. Mya zipped up her suitcase and walked over to their dresser. "I guess we're even now," she laughed, taking her wedding ring off and placing it on the dresser. "I'll send for the rest of my things later this week." With that, Mya turned and walked out the room. "Fuck!" King yelled out once she was gone. He looked down and noticed the envelope with the photos still sitting on the bed. King picked up the photos and slowly flipped through them. Star had managed to take the pictures from the perfect angle. The first picture showed her lips wrapped snugly around his piece while he gripped the back of head with his head thrown back in pleasure. In the second photo, Star was bent over the bed while King held her waist from behind plowing in and out of her. From the photos, it was obvious, King was enjoying every moment of their sex session. King ripped the pictures in half and threw them on the floor. He jumped off the bed and rushed over to the closet to grab an outfit to throw on. It was time he paid that bitch Star a visit. King tried to calm himself down on the ride over to Star's house. But the more he thought about the night that landed him in this situation, the angrier he became. Star sat in the corner of the bar and watched King as he took shot after shot, lost in his own thoughts. The women in the bar were like vultures and could smell when a man wasn't happy at home. King was a hood legend and women had no shame making it known they were willing to play any position he allowed them too, just to be a part of his team. Star laughed to herself as King waved off woman after woman that approached him. It would take more than just a fat ass to get a man like King, Star knew because she had been waving hers in his face for over a year now with no luck. After his tenth shot, the barmaid Maria cut off King's drinks. She was close friends with King's mother and had known King for his entire life. Maria refused to play a part in him having an accident on the way home because he was drunk. "That's enough big guy," she said, removing the empty shot glasses from in front of him. Marie knew something was bothering King because he wasn't his normal cheerful self but decided not to pry. Her main concern was him to make it home safely. Patting him on the hand, Marie told King to come back tomorrow and take care of his tab. She didn't want him pulling out a wad of money in the bar while he was tipsy. King stood up and kissed the older lady on the cheek. "I owe you!" He walked out of the bar and was thankful to feel the fresh air. He didn't realize how tipsy he was until he stood up. Making it to his car King dropped his keys while trying to unlock the door. A peep toe red bottom heel stepped on top of the keys as he bent down to pick them up. "You really shouldn't be driving in that condition," a voice said. King raised his head and came face to face with Star. He grunted in anger. "Move bitch," he said giving Star a shove to remove her feet off his keys. "You have turned my wife into a lying hoe just like you," he yelled. Star laughed on the inside. So, her plan had worked after all. King almost fell over when he bent down again to pick up his keys. "I'm not letting you drive like this," Star said snatching the keys off the ground before King could reach them. Hitting unlock on King's car doors, Star slid into the driver's seat. "Either get in or call an Uber," she told him while starting up the car. King already had a pending case and he didn't need to add a DUI to his list of charges. He walked around the car and jumped in the passenger seat. Star laughed at him sitting there sulking like a kid. Before they could pull out the parking lot King had nodded off to sleep. Mya drove quietly making sure not to wake him before they reached their destination. Twenty minutes later, Mya pulled up to the Embassy Suites in Dearborn and dashed in. She was happy to see King still knocked out in the front seat when she returned. King opened his eyes to the feel of someone lightly shaking him. He blinked his eyes a few times trying to remember how he had left the bar. "After what you said about Mya back at the bar, I didn't think you wanted to be driven home," Star innocently said while holding out the room card. She had to play her role perfectly if she wanted her plan to work. Snatching the key from her hand, King starting walking in the direction of the hotel room. The number of shots King had taken at the bar was pressing against his bladder. He didn't have time to stand outside and argue with Star. He would have locked Star out the hotel room, but she still had his car keys. When King emerged from the bathroom Star was sitting on the bed, with her jacket and shoes off. "Isn't it about time you go fuck somebody for your next meal?" he spat while grabbing the remote control off the dresser and flopping down on the bed. "I'm about too," she laughed. Standing up, Star slid the dress she was wearing over her head revealing her nude body underneath. The sight of her perky titties, wide hips, and plump ass had King instantly hard. King and Mya hadn't had sex in weeks. When Star saw the look of lust in his eyes she slowly walked over and stood in front of him. "You like what you see daddy?" she sexily said while caressing her nipples. Star leaned in and rubbed her perky titties across King's lips. The feel of King's lips against her skin sent an electric shock through her body causing her juices to run down her leg. King reached down in between Star's legs and roughly rubbed. He slightly moaned at the feel of how wet she was. King didn't know if it was the alcohol or his anger toward Mya that didn't make him stop. Star lowered her body to her knees and rubbed King's hardness through his jeans impressed with the size. She stuck her hands down in his jeans and lightly stroked him before pulling out his chocolate stick. Star's mouth watered at the beautiful, thick, long piece in front of her. She spit on it twice before taking it fully in her mouth. King's toes curled and mouth dropped wide open at the feel of Star's warm mouth. He watched in amazement as she switched from swallowing him whole, to licking up and down his shaft. King had been orally pleased by a lot of women, but none had ever given him a blow job this good. He now understood how she was able to pay all her high ass bills so easy. King grabbed Star by the hair and pushed her down further on him. The sound of her gagging and choking was turning him on. "Suck that dick," he barked. When King felt himself about to cum, he didn't bother to tell Star. He held her head still as he came down her throat. Star happily swallowed all King's seeds. King pulled his still hard dick from Star's mouth and yanked her up roughly by her hair. Bending her over the bed, he forcefully rammed inside her. King was surprised at how tight she felt after all the men she had been with. Star came the minute King slid inside her. She tried to keep her balance as her body shook from her orgasm and King pumping in and out of her at the same time. She made her ass clap and jiggle while throwing it back. King's loud grunts let Star know Mya wasn't putting it on him like she was. Star lost count of how many orgasms ripped through her body from the pounding King was putting on her pussy. He snatched Star's head back while roughly slapping her on the ass. The sight of his large red handprints on Star's huge yellow ass every time he smacked it, had him ready to cum again. King closed his eyes and got lost in Star's tightness and warmth. "Damn Mya," he yelled out as he came. When he opened his eyes, King saw Star, not Mya looking back at him smiling. King looked down in disgust, watching his semen drip out of her. "Get out," he spat. Star laughed as she slipped her dress back on. She had just got what she wanted, and maybe more. Star sat on her couch tipsy from the bottle of liquor she had been drinking all day. She tried to tune out the constant ringing of her doorbell, but whoever was at the door would not go away. Star stumbled over the half empty bottle of Cîroc as she stood up and headed toward the door. Star was so drunk, that she didn't care about being completely naked as she flung the door open and came face to face with King. The cold look in his eyes told Star that Mya had saw the pictures she sent in the mail. Before she could slam the door shut, King pushed his way inside the house and slammed the door behind him. Grabbing Star by the hair, he dragged her over to the couch and roughly shoved her down. "You are a jealous devious bitch," he roared, mushing Star upside the head. King raised his fist but immediately dropped it when an image of his mother popped into his head. No matter how mad he was at the moment, King could never bring himself to hitting a woman. Not even a bitch like Star, who deserved it. When King looked down and saw Star crying, he wondered how she could be the same cold-hearted person who hated her so called "best friend" to the point of trying to ruin her life. "I tried to warn Mya about you," King laughed while flopping down next to Star on the couch and picking up the half empty bottle of Cîroc off the floor. "I probably should have been warning myself," he laughed while taking a long swig out the bottle. King sat quietly on the couch and finished off the bottle of liquor, enjoying the buzz he was feeling. Anything was better than facing the reality that he had probably lost Mya forever. "Why?" King slurred as he turned to look at Star. That was a question Star couldn't really answer. She had been filled with hate for so long that she didn't know how to recognize genuine love. Star didn't hate Mya, she hated what Mya represented. Mya was confident, smart, and went after the things she wanted in life the right way. Those were all qualities Star didn't possess. She knew once Don found out what happened between her and King, they would be over. Just when things were looking up in Star's life everything began crashing down because of her own jealous actions. King noticed for the first time Star was sitting on the couch completely nude and couldn't fight off the lust that filled his body thinking of their last encounter. He tried to blame his desires on the liquor, but the truth was he was a man and like most men he was letting his "little head" instead of his big head think for him. King leaned over and began roughly kissing Star. He enjoyed the tart taste of alcohol on her breath as his tongue explored her mouth. When Star began kissing him back King knew there was no turning back. Star was surprised when King began kissing her and as much as she knew they were wrong for what they were doing she couldn't resist. Pulling her into his lap, King fondled and massaged her breasts. He gently squeezed her nipples before sucking on them one at a time. King reached under Star and pulled his hard manhood loose from his jogging pants. Star lifted her body up and slid down King's pole inch by inch. King placed his large hands on each side of her waist and guided her motions and she rotated her hips back and forth. "Damn," he grunted at the feel of her warmness. When Star's body began to vibrate from an orgasm, King exploded as well. Sweaty and out of breath, King pushed Star off him. "We can't do this again. We have to tell Don," he said. Shaking his head, King stuffed himself back into his pants and walked out the door. Star was poison and King had been bitten.

Chapter 2

MYA

Mya laid across the bed in her mother's guest bedroom and stared up at the ceiling in a daze. She didn't bother to turn her head and look in her mother's direction when she heard her walk into the room. Mya had spent the last two weeks hiding out at her mother's and refusing to talk to anyone. She felt betrayed and deceived in the worst way. True enough she had secretly aborted her and King's baby, but that was only because she thought King was cheating. Mya honestly didn't feel like her actions justified King sleeping with her best friend. Looking back Mya had to admit she did overlook a lot of things about Star that she should not have. Star and Mya were best friend for years, yet Mya didn't truly know anything about her. Mya had never met any of Star's family and Star rarely talked about her past. Whenever Mya would try to bring up anything about Star's family, she would become angry and defensive. That should have been a red flag to Mya but because she truly loved Star, Mya ignored all the warning signs of Star's potential backstabbing ways. Mya's mother sat on the side of the bed and gently pulled her daughter into her arms. Mya let all her emotions out as she sobbed like a little girl. "Shh! Baby, it's okay," her mother said. "How could they do this to me?" Mya wailed. Mya's mother was not surprised at all by Star's behavior. She felt like Star was a snake from the first day she met her. But she was shocked, to say the least, by King. Her mother felt like it was more to the story and decided now was the time to figure out what happened. Mya's mother gently eased her daughter out of her arms and looked her in the eyes. "Did something happen that you're not telling me about?" she asked. When Mya looked down at the bed, her mother knew she was right. "I had an abortion without telling King I was pregnant. Mya's mother gasped in shock. "MYA!" she shrieked. She never thought her daughter would do something so cruel. She wanted to scold Mya but knew now wasn't the time. While she still didn't excuse the fact of King and Star sleeping together, at least now she had reasoning behind King's behavior. King was a man acting out of hurt. "Baby, one act of betrayal only leads to a thousand more. That was that man's child too. He had every right to be included in that decision," Mya's mother said in a voice full of disappointment. Mya sat quietly and listened to her mother's words. If she could turn back the hands of time, she would.

****

After staying with her mother for a few weeks, Mya was tired of the pity party. What was done was done. It was time for Mya to move on. She hadn't talked to King since the day she stormed out of their house, although he called her repeatedly. Mya wasn't ready to talk yet and probably wouldn't be ready anytime soon. She wasn't going to go as far as filing for a divorce from King, but she certainly wasn't going to go running right back. Mya brought home a nice six-figure income as a financial advisor and could easily afford a place on her own. She located a beautiful, small, three-bedroom brick condominium right outside the city and immediately fell in love. After a little negotiating, Mya wrote out a check to cover the full amount of her new home and handed it to the real estate agent. The real estate agent thanked Mya and headed out. Mya locked up her new home, jumped into her car and headed back to her mother's house. First thing tomorrow morning she would go pick out new furniture. "Out with the old and in with the new," Mya said out loud while searching though her Apple music selection on her phone looking for the perfect album to enjoy during her drive. She turned the volume of the radio all the way up when I Bet by Ciara came on. Singing along with the music, Mya couldn't stop the tears from falling down her face. I bet you start loving me as soon as I start loving someone else Somebody better than you And I know that it hurts, you know that it hurts your pride But you thought the grass was greener on the other side I bet you start loving me as soon as I start loving someone else Somebody better than you.

Chapter 3

DON

Don sat on his patio smoking a cigar with a worried look on his face. He had been trying to get in touch with Star for over a week now with no luck. Scrolling through his phone and looking at their last text message Don was confused. He had just told Star that he loved her and was giving her the title as his wifey. Why would she just up and disappear on him? Don dialed Star's number again. When her voicemail picked for the millionth time, he hung up. Deciding to drive by Star's house, Don jumped up and grabbed his car keys before heading out the door. After driving by Star's house and not seeing her car outside Don decided to give Mya a call to see if she knew where Star could be. Normally Don would have called King first, but knowing how his partner felt about Star, Don felt he could get more accurate information from Mya, being that she was Star's best friend. Sitting in Star's driveway, Don rolled up a blunt of Kush before dialing Mya's number. He needed something to relax his mind. "Hello?" Mya curiously answered wondering why Don was calling her phone. "Hey sis, I'm trying to find Star. Do you have any idea where she may be?" Mya pulled the phone away from her ear like it had just bit her. Placing the phone back to her ear Mya asked, "Why the fuck would I know where that bitch is at?" Don dropped the blunt he was inhaling, just barely missing burning the Italian leather seats of the luxury car. Don was shocked to hear Mya cuss and even more surprised to hear her call Star out her name. Don brushed the ashes off his seat. "Am I missing something?" he asked confused. It hit Mya that Don didn't have a clue about everything going on. "Where are you?" Mya asked. "I'm sitting in Star's driveway." Mya told Don they needed to talk face to face and gave him her address. A million questions were going through Don's head. Why was Mya living in a different house than her and King's? Where the hell was King? Don hadn't tried to contact his boy since their meeting at the lawyer's office last week because he assumed King and Mya were in Hawaii celebrating their one-year anniversary, but now he knew that wasn't the case. But if King wasn't in Hawaii why hadn't he reached out to Don and let him know he was still in town. Don's body filled with dread as he started up his car. Something told him that he wasn't going to like the answers to all his questions. Don could have sworn he saw the blinds slightly move as he took one last look at Star's dark house before pulling off. "Maybe this weed has me tripping," he mumbled, while backing out of the driveway.

****

Mya was unsure of why Don was looking for Star in the first place. From what she knew, the two could hardly stand each other. Suddenly, Mya laughed at that thought. There was a time that she thought King and Star could hardly stand each other as well. Mya went into her fully stocked pantry and grabbed a bottle of cognac for Don, and a bottle of wine for her. She already knew this was going to be a long night. Pouring herself a glass of wine, Mya got comfortable on the couch and turned on the latest episode of Love and Hip Hop while she waited on Don to arrive. It felt good to focus on someone else's drama for a change. Mya was just getting into the show when her doorbell rang. Turning the volume on the television down, Mya went to the door and let Don in. "Hey sis," Don said, bending down to give Mya a kiss on the cheek. Mya could tell by the look on Don's face he was nervous about what she had to say. Don followed Mya into the living room and noticed the bottle of cognac and a bottle of wine sitting on the coffee table. "That bad huh?" he lightly chuckled while pouring himself a double shot of the cognac. "Unfortunately!" Mya sadly said, refilling her glass of wine. Mya grabbed her phone off the table and punched in her passcode. Mya scrolled through her photo gallery and stopped on the snapshots of King and Star that she was looking for. She handed her phone to Don; thankful she had thought to snap a few pictures of the photos and save them in her phone before confronting King with them. "What the fuck," Don screamed loud enough for Mya's neighbors to hear. "Is this some type of sick joke?" he whispered in disbelief. "I wish it was," Mya whispered. Don stared at the picture of Star bent over a bed in a hotel room with King sliding into her from behind. Don and King had been best friends since the sandbox. King was the only person Don trusted with his life. Never in a million years would Don have imagined

King would betray him or Mya like this. At first Mya thought Don was in shock that King had betrayed her. But the more she looked into Don's eyes while he stared at the phone, Mya could see his hurt went much deeper. "Don, why were you looking for Star earlier?" Mya calmly asked. Don hesitated before answering. Admitting why he was looking for Star, would be admitting that he had allowed himself to be deceived into thinking he could turn a hoe into a housewife. Mya's hands flew over her mouth. "You were fucking her, weren't you?" she screeched, slowly putting all the pieces of the puzzle together. When Don dropped his head into his hands Mya knew the answer to her question. "Did King know?" she wondered out loud. Don shook his head no. Pouring himself another shot, Don sat back on the couch and mentally went over everything he just learned. So, Star wasn't missing after all, she was hiding from him. Hiding from her deceit and betrayal. "So, what now?" he asked, looking over at Mya. When Mya began sobbing loudly, Don pulled her into his arms and gently stroked her hair. "It's going to be okay," he soothingly said. Mya laid in Don's arms enjoying the warm feeling of his arms wrapped around her body. Caught up in the moment, Mya reached up and placed a soft kiss on Don's lip. Don softly parted her lips with his tongue and hungrily explored the inside of her mouth. As their tongues found a beautiful rhythm, Mya knew they had both just crossed a line there was no going back from. Don gently pushed Mya back on the couch and anxiously pulled the thin maxi dress she was wearing over her head. He gently sucked her hardened chocolate nipples causing her to moan out in delight. Don trailed kissed down her soft chocolate skin until he reached her neatly shaved peach. Placing one of Mya's legs on his shoulders, Don separated her lower lips with his tongue. He licked and sucked on her pearl causing Mya to squeal out in pure delight. Mya played with her nipples and became hypnotized looking at Don's deep waves on the top of his head as she watched his head move back and forth between her legs. "Shit," Mya hissed. Don was giving her the best head of her life. Because King had been Mya's first partner, she assumed everything he did in bed was the best, but that was because she had nothing to compare him with. The sensations Don's tongue was sending through her body caused Mya to realize how wrong she had been. When Don felt Mya's legs begin to quiver he tightened his grip on her hips. Her juices tasted so sweet he wanted to savor every drop. After two back to back powerful organisms Mya legs were completely numb. Mya laid in a state of bliss as Don stood up and pulled off his jeans and boxers. "Are you sure you want to do this?" he asked Mya while easing himself back down on top of her. When Mya reached down and grabbed his erection to guide him into her, that was all the answer he needed. Don slowly glided in and out of Mya enjoying the feel of her warmth. "Damn this shit good," Don moaned. He couldn't help but to wonder what would make King cheat on Mya with Star. Mya was the type of woman every man dreamed about. She had a good head on her shoulders and good pussy between her legs. What else could a man ask for? They both moaned out in pleasure as their pain of betrayal turned into passion. Don slowed his strokes and enjoyed the feel of Mya's soft lips against his skin as she nibbled and sucked on his neck. Don lifted Mya's thick legs in the air and plunged deep inside her. Mya's walls were so tight they felt like a vacuum around his manhood. Never losing his stroke Don placed Mya's freshly manicured toes into his mouth and gently sucked them one by one causing Mya's eyes to roll in the back of head. "Ohhhhhh... My... GGGGod," Mya stuttered as Don sent her body into convulsions. Don looked down and stared into Mya's beautiful eyes that were filled with pain and lust. Don felt his thighs tighten up as tingling sensations shot from his toes to his stomach. He wanted to pull out, but the warmth and tightness of Mya's walls had a hold on him. Grabbing Mya by the hips Don growled like an animal as he released himself deep into her. Don collapsed on top of Mya and they laid on the couch in an awkward silence for a few minutes before Mya jumped off the couch, grabbed her nightgown off the floor and ran into the bathroom. The reality of what she just did hit her like a ton of bricks, as Don's warm semen ran down her thigh. "Did I really just sleep with my husband's best friend?" For a moment Mya felt bad. "What goes around comes around," she smirked while turning on the warm water in the sink for a quick "hoe bath." Mya finished cleaning herself up and came out the bathroom where she found Don sitting on the couch staring off into space. Mya handed him a warm soapy washcloth to clean himself off. They looked at each other and both said, "This never happened," simultaneously.

Chapter 4

KING

King sat behind his custom cherrywood desk rocking back and forth in the plush, leather swivel chair. He missed Mya something terrible. King was glad Mya still called and talked to his mother so he could stay up to date on what was going on in her life. He wasn't shocked when his mother told him Mya had purchased her a house already. King knew Mya could easily hold her own financially. That was one of the things he loved most about her, she was very independent. King left money with his mother on several occasions to give to Mya, but she refused. At this point King was losing hope that he would ever be able to get his wife back. Picking up his phone King dialed Don's number. He hadn't spoken to his partner in a few weeks out of guilt. King was ready to get everything off his chest and hope his friend would forgive him. Don was in the middle of his daily workout when his phone began to ring. He was surprised when he looked down and saw King's name flash across the screen. For weeks he'd debated if he was going to confront King about the information Mya had given him but decided against it. Don was hurt by King's actions, but he would still ride for King in a heartbeat if he needed him. He slowed down the speed of the treadmill and answered the phone. "What's up?" Don grunted into the phone when he answered it. King and Don had been friends for years and King could always tell right away when something was bothering his man. By the tone of Don's voice King figured he already knew about everything that happened between him and Star. "We need to talk bro," King flatly said, getting right to the point. "I'll meet you at our regular spot in an hour," Don responded before hanging up. The two had lived by their number one rule "Money Over Bitches" for years and nothing was going to change that. Not even Star's devious ass. Anxious to hear what King had to say Don cut his workout short and headed to the shower. Thoughts of Mya invaded his head as Don soaped up his body. He felt his dick stiffen up remembering how snuggly her walls fit around him. He stroked his erection with his soapy hand while picturing Mya's chocolate thick legs propped up on his shoulders. Don grabbed the shower rod with his free hand to catch himself from falling as he watched his seeds spill out his body and down the shower drain. By the time Don got out of the shower he was relaxed and ready to let bygones be bygones with King "if" he said the right thing. As far as Don was concerned, they were now even. Don threw on a pair of Robin jeans with the matching t-shirt. After brushing his waves a few times and slipping his iced out Rolex around his wrist, Don headed out the door. He was ready to get this conversation with King over and done with. King was already sitting in the back of Tereasa's, when Don came casually strolling through the door. It took Don a minute to reach the table because every few steps he took, a man was either giving him a dap or a woman was leaning in for a hug. Tereasa's was the Detroit hood version of Cheers. A place you go where everyone knows your name. King and Don were regulars at the bar, and it wasn't uncommon for them to pick up the tab for a random group of pretty ladies drinking in the bar. When Don finally made it to the table where King was waiting, he flagged the thick, caramel complexion waitress over and ordered a platter of chicken wings with four double shots of Hennessy. "What's up stranger," Don sarcastically said taking in his friend's wore down appearance. "I see it's no need of beating around the bush," King said. "I guess you already know I fucked Star, huh?" King smirked. King could tell from Don's stand-offish demeanor his boy was feeling some type of way. Before Don could respond the waitress came over and brought their food and drinks. Don slid two of the double shots in front of King before taking a swig of one of the shots in front of him. "All I want to know is did you fuck Star before or after I told you I was going to wife her?" Don asked, looking King square in the eyes. "Before. Look bro, I had no idea you and Star had something going on," I had just found out Mya had an abortion while we were out of town squaring up our tab with the connect. She never even told me she was pregnant. She thought I was cheating because of how much time I was spending away from home moving the rest of the product we had left," King sadly said, thinking about the day he discovered Mya's betrayal. King told Mya to relax while he went downstairs and fixed her some soup. After he poured the soup in a pot, and cut it on low, King grabbed his phone to check his messages and voicemails. He realized the phone hadn't been powered back on since leaving his connect's estate earlier. Waiting on the phone to cut on, King stirred Mya's soup, making sure it didn't burn. He punched in his password and scanned through the large number of missed calls and messages. He noticed several messages from an unknown number. When he opened the first message his heart nearly jumped out of his chest. There was a picture of Mya walking into an abortion clinic, with the words, "Guess she not so perfect after all," attached to the image. King took his fingers and enlarged the photo. That was definitely Mya in the photo, and he knew the picture was recent because she was wearing the Nike outfit, he had just purchased from the mall for her the other day. King turned the soup off and stormed up the stairs. There had to be some type of logical explanation for this. "The soup done already bae?" Mya's head was tilted back on the pillow with her eyes closed. When King didn't respond, Mya opened her eyes and looked in his direction. The look on his face, froze her in fear. "Tell me you didn't abort our baby," he stated in a calm, flat tone. The calmness in King's voice sent shivers down her spine. Mya wanted to say no, but by the look on King's face, she knew he already knew the truth, so it was no point in lying. "I can explain," she whispered. King punched the wall, leaving a huge hole the size of his fist. "Yes or fuckin no!" he screamed. "I thought you were cheating," she sobbed. "So instead of being a woman, a wife, and coming to me, you ran off and killed our child." King's words stung, because Mya knew he was right. "You more of a conniving bitch than Star. Guess birds of a feather really do flock together," he laughed, before storming out the house. Don's mouthed dropped open in surprise. He would never have imagined Mya would do something so scandalous. Don's body filled with guilt as he thought about what he and Mya had done. "Damn," he fucked his right-hand man, his brother, his best friend's wife off some bullshit information. Don wouldn't even be surprised if Star was somehow behind King finding out about Mya's secret abortion. Don originally planned on coming clean with King about sleeping with Mya, but he couldn't do that now. The more he thought about what he did, the more disloyal Don felt. Star was a jump off, and Don knew that from the start. He should not have been surprised by her behavior. Mya was King's wife and should have been off limits, period. He just prayed Mya would hold up to her end of the bargain and take their secret to her grave. "It wasn't your fault," Don said. "I should have told you I was seeing Star instead of trying to keep it a secret. I know you would have never betrayed me like that if you knew she was my girl." King cringed at Don's word. The last time he indulged in Star's goodies, King knew that Don was in love with her and just didn't care. He decided to leave that small detail out. What Don didn't know wouldn't hurt him. "So, we good?" King raised an eyebrow and asked. "Money over Bitches," Don said while raising his glass. For the rest of the night the two men went over their legal situation. It was now time for them to focus on what was important, their freedom!

Chapter 5

RICHARD (KING AND DON'S LAWYER)

King and Don's lawyer Richard sat in his office tapping away on his computer busily preparing his notes for court tomorrow. He made a mental note to hire a new secretary as soon as possible. "If Richard could only stop sleeping with every secretary he hired, they might stick around," he chuckled to himself. As a senior partner in one of Detroit most prestigious law firms, Richard had it all. A beautiful home, several luxury cars, an obedient wife, and a beautiful mistress on the side. Well he "DID" have a beautiful mistress on the side. Richard grimaced as he thought about Star. It was because of Star that Richard had made senior partner. After flaunting her around at company parties Richard's boss came to him with an offer he couldn't refuse. If Richard agreed to "rent out" Star to his boss for one night, he would be guaranteed a promotion within the law firm. One night turned into many as Richard offered Star to several more senior partners as he climbed the corporate ladder, eventually making senior partner. Richard kept Star in a luxurious condo and laced in the most expensive clothes and jewelry money could buy and in return Star only had to keep her mouth closed and legs open. Their arrangement was working out great until Star fell in love with Don, a low life drug dealer who turned out to be one of Richard's clients. Anger consumed his body thinking about the day he overheard King and Don talking about Star. By the time King reached the lawyer's office, Don and their lawyer Richard were already going over the case. "Sorry I'm late guys," he said. King stared at Richard for a few minutes trying to remember where he knew him from. It will come back to me, he thought before grabbing a seat. Over the next two hours Don, King, and Richard went over the Feds' potential case against them. "Maybe it is not as bad as we think," Don said while pulling his phone out to check his messages. He smiled as he opened the message from Star. She was laid across her bed naked and covered in the flowers he left on her porch that morning. "If I didn't know better, I would think you were in love my nigga," King teased laughing at Don blushing at his phone. Don quickly typed in, "See you soon wifey!" and sent the message before sitting his phone on Richard's desk to put on his jacket. "I guess now is a good time to tell you. I am in love bro, with Star." "Star," King yelled. Don hoped King would understand but he was going to make Star his wifey whether King understood or not. "Man, I know how you feel about her, but I'm telling you, I think she has changed," Don said. King dropped his head. Less than twenty-four hours ago, he had his dick touching the back of the woman his best friend loved throat plus she was also his wife's best friend. King had fucked up royally. Feeling Richard's eyes on them, Don asked King to step into the hallway so they could finish their conversation in private. Richard stood there in silence as the men exited the room. Was it possible that Don was talking about his Star? Noticing Don had left his phone on the desk Richard quickly picked it up and breathed a sigh of relief that the phone was not locked. Hitting a few buttons, he went to the last message in Don's phone. His body shook in anger, as a picture of Star's naked body came across the screen.

Now he understood why Star had been ignoring his calls and requests to see her lately. "That ungrateful bitch," he fumed. After all he had done for her, paid her rent, brought her expensive jewelry, even putting her gold-digging ass through college because her crackhead mother couldn't afford her tuition. For her to just up and leave him for a low life drug dealer. Richard let out a sinister laugh, exiting out the message and placing Don's phone back on the desk. Richard smirked as he reached into his bottom drawer and pulled out King and Don's file. According to one of his inside sources, King and Don would be arrested any day now. After going over their case notes, Richard ran across one huge mistake the prosecutor's office made when putting King and Don's case together. A mistake that would cost them their case "IF" it ever came to light. Richard's law firm took great pride in the high number of cases their office was able to get dismissed for their clients. Every attorney within the law office went above and beyond to find any evidence or any small technicality they could to possibly get their clients off, including hiring the best private investigators money could buy. Richard was like a little kid in the candy store when he originally received the call he was waiting for, from the private investigator he put on Don and King's case. Their private investigators only called when they had vital information that could break the case. Richard listened intently as the private investigator told him about "the informant," whose information the entire prosecutor's case was built on turned out to be one of the cousins of a federal agent working on the case. Richard highly doubted if either man was aware of this because they were distant cousins who grew up in different states but whether the agent knew or not didn't matter. Guess it was a small world after all, Richard laughed. Richard knew this was a loophole that could get King and Don's whole case thrown out. Unfortunately for Don and King this information would never be disclosed to anyone. Richard scanned over the information one last time before he closed the folder and threw it inside his briefcase. He made a mental note to shred the documents on his personal shredder once he made it home. For the past few weeks Star had been ignoring all of Richard's calls and he knew that was only because of her new love interest Mr. Don. Richard knew the only way to get Star fully back into his life was by getting rid of Don, and that's exactly what he planned to do. Richard smiled as he shut down his computer for the day. Grabbing his jacket off the back of the chair Richard headed home. He needed to spend as much quality time as possible with his wife over the next few days. Soon Don would be locked up and Star would come crawling back and receiving all his attention.

Chapter 6

STAR

"Shit! Shit! Shit!" Star screamed looking down at the pregnancy test she was holding in her trembling hand. Star was so stressed out with everything going on she didn't realize she had missed her period last month until she went into her linen closet in search of something and noticed the half empty box of tampons sitting on the shelf. Star grabbed the box of tampons off the shelf and tried to remember when the last time was, she used them. When she couldn't pinpoint an exact date, Star grabbed her car keys off the dresser and rushed two blocks over to the pharmacy. Grabbing two different pregnancy tests, Star waiting impatiently in line while the ghetto clerk behind the counter loudly smacked on her gum and sang along to the music blaring over the store speakers. When Star finally made it to the front of the line, she threw her money on the counter and didn't bother to wait on any change. Star rushed back home and hurried to the bathroom. She squatted over the toilet and struggled to pee directly on the small white stick because her hands were shaking so bad. Placing the test on the edge of the counter she nervously paced the floor back and forth while she waited. It took less than one minute for two bright pink lines to pop up on the stick. Star slowly slid down the bathroom door and cried. For the first time in years she felt completely alone. She knew Mya probably hated her for what she had done and honestly Star couldn't blame her. Star hadn't heard from King since the day he left her house and she was too afraid to try and call Don. In a daze Star searched through her phone and found the number to her doctor's office. After making an appointment for the next day, Star crawled into bed and rubbed her stomach that was just starting to slightly protrude and sighed. Sadly, Star had no clue who her child's father was because she had slept with Don and King unprotected within days of each other. Thankfully Star and Richard hadn't slept together in months so she could factor him out as a possibility. She cringed thinking about all the awful things she did over the last few years. To most people from the outside looking in Star appeared to be a beautiful and confident woman living her best life. A life most people only dreamed about. Looking at Star's outer beauty no one could imagine the inner mental and emotional scars. They didn't see all the insecurities that Star hid behind her lavish lifestyle. Since the day Star and Mya met back in college, the two instantly became best friends. While Mya was a loving and devoted friend to Star, Star secretly envied Mya. Most people would have been happy over their friend's success, but Mya's perfect life was a constant reminder to Star of how imperfect her life was. If Star wasn't so busy trying to find any reason to hate Mya, she would have understood Mya's constant criticism of her behavior was only out of love because she just wanted the best for her. That was hard for Star to understand because of the toxic relationship she had with her own mother. Star's mother was a crackhead who spent more time turning tricks for her next hit than loving and nurturing her own daughter. Because Star was never shown any real love as a child, she didn't know how to give or receive it. Star's original plan was to trick King into sleeping with her in hopes of ruining his and Mya marriage. But after falling in love with King's best friend Don, Star had a change of heart. That was until Don rejected her. Now here she was pregnant with two best friends who could possibly be the daddy. The thought alone made Star cringe at the realization of how low she had stooped. Regardless of her current situation, having an abortion was out of the question for her. Star's body had already withstood several abortions over the years, and she feared this may be her last chance at motherhood. Star prayed Don turned out to be the father of her unborn child. Over the last few weeks Star realized how much she loved him. When the constant phone calls and pop up visits from Don suddenly stopped last week, Star guessed Don somehow found out what happened between her and King. Star loved Don and prayed sharing a child together would make Don forgive her and bring them back together. She tossed and turned all night anxious about her doctor's visit tomorrow. The next morning Star woke up early and fixed herself a light breakfast of turkey bacon, scrambled eggs, and toast. After cleaning up the kitchen Star jumped in the shower and quickly lathered down her body. Standing in her huge walk-in closet she decided on a cute maxi dress that accented her curves. It wouldn't be long before she started fully showing so she might as well enjoy her figure while she could. Grabbing her purse and keys off the dresser, Star rushed out the door. Her mind was racing with so many thoughts as she backed out the driveway, Star didn't pay attention to the black car with dark tinted windows sitting a few doors down from her house as she sped past. Star shivered as the doctor spread the cool gel across her belly. "Sorry," the petite Asian doctor giggled as she turned her attention toward the monitor. The room was eerily quiet except for the loud water sound coming from the ultrasound machine Star was hooked up to. Her heart raced staring into the concerned doctors face. "Oh My God. Is my baby okay?" Star asked in a panic voice. Before the doctor could respond the beautiful sound of Star's baby heartbeat filled the room. Tears of joy slid down Star face at the beautiful sound. "I'm going to be a mother," she whispered. The doctor smiled down at her "Yes you are. According to this you are two months along." Star smile faded when she realized that meant King or Don could be her child father. If she was a little further along, she could be sure Don was the father. She and Don were having unprotected sex for at least a month before she slept with King. Two months ago, she slept with Don and King within days of each other. The only way she could be sure who her baby father was would be through a DNA test. She thanked the doctor and stopped by the receptionist's desk to set up her next appointment. Looking down into her purse and digging around for her keys, Star yanked them out anxious to get back home. She hit the unlock button on her keypad and gasped. All four of her car tires had been slashed and the word slut was carved in the driver's side door. Star looked around while protectively clutching her stomach. She turned and ran back into the doctor's office screaming for help.

Chapter 7

MYA

Mya was comfortably adjusting to the single life. While she did miss King, Mya wasn't sure if she wanted to stay married to him. They both had betrayed each other's trust almost beyond repair. The thin silk panties Mya wore under her linen suit became damp as she thought about James' long, thick tongue and dick. James was one of Mya's students in the financial investment class she taught once a week. After inviting Mya out for drinks one night after class, one thing led to another and Mya found herself letting him lick her kitty into an orgasmic coma on a regular basis. Mya walked over to her office door and locked it. She dug into her purse and pulled out the small gold case that could easily be mistaken for a wallet. Mya popped the case open and pulled out her favorite tiny pink vibrator with the pearl tip. Mya slid her panties to the side and positioned one leg on top of her desk. She placed the vibrator against her clit and began to rotate it in a circular motion imagining it was James' tongue. Mya began breathing heavy and bit down on her lip to keep from screaming out as the orgasm ripped through her body. She enjoyed the tingling sensations rolling through her body for a few minutes before throwing the vibrator back in her purse, grabbing some Kleenex out her desk, and cleaning herself off. Mya laughed to herself, thinking if someone had told her she would be masturbating under her desk in the middle of the day a year ago, she would have called them crazy. Before meeting King, Mya was an innocent virgin that knew nothing about sex. Being single over the last few months caused Mya to begin exploring her body more and becoming more in tune with her sensual side. Mya knew she had to decide sooner rather than later if she was willing to give King a second chance. Her and James hadn't engaged in intercourse yet, but she knew it was only so long before her body craved for more than just James' lips and tongue. Mya's thoughts drifted to Don. He was the only man who had dipped his stick in her goodies besides King. She wondered if Don would be willing to dick her down one more good time. She giggled to herself at the naughty thought. King had his fun, why shouldn't she? Mya clicked on her computer and tapped her nails on the desk while she waited for it to boot up. Her eyes roamed around her desk and landed on the picture of her and Star on their college graduation day. A twinge of pain tugged at Mya's heart as she thought about her ex-best friend. Mya both loved and hated Star right now. For years Mya had tried to be the best friend she could be to Star only to get stabbed in the back. Mya could kick herself for ignoring the constant ridicule and sarcastic remarks made by Star on a regular basis. The whole time Mya looked at Star like a sister, Star wanted to take her place. Mya didn't hate Star, but she would never trust or befriend her again. She was slightly more open to forgiving King because she knew he had only acted out of hurt. If Mya never would have secretly snuck off and aborted King's baby, he would have never been vulnerable that night in the first place. King made a bad decision in the heat of the moment, while Star had been plotting on how to destroy Mya for a while. That type of hate was dangerous. Mya figured if she made King suffer enough, he wouldn't make the same mistake again.

Star was a different story. She was a snake by heart and like her mother always said, "No matter how nice you are to a snake; they are still a snake and will bite you any chance they get!" Mya snatched the photo of her and Star off the desk and threw it in the bottom drawer. She didn't need any more distractions for the day. Mya was a financial advisor for one of the top consultant companies in Michigan. She had back to back appointments scheduled for the rest of the day and if everything went according to plan a lot of zeros would be added to her already growing bank account. Since their separation King sent flowers to Mya's job once a week with a ten-thousand-dollar check attached for her weekly expenses. King knew Mya didn't need the money, but he was trying to do anything he could to show Mya he was sorry in hopes of getting his wife back. Mya didn't spend a dime of King's money. Instead she opened a separate bank account where she deposited his checks. Mya was determined to show King she didn't need anything from him but his love and loyalty.

****

Mya was just wrapping up her last meeting for the day when her assistant Tiffany came barging through her office door holding her iPad in her hands with a look of panic on her face. Mya knew whatever Tiffany had to say must have been serious for her to interrupt Mya's meetings. Mya's client stood and promised her he would be sending over a signed contract first thing tomorrow to secure her services while he hurriedly gathered up his belongings to give the ladies some privacy, sensing that something was wrong. Once Mya's client walked out the door Tiffany rushed over and closed the door behind him. When Tiffany told Mya, she might want to sit down, Mya's heart sunk down into her stomach. Tiffany hit a few buttons on her iPad and turned the screen in Mya's direction. Mya's hand flew over her mouth as an image of King in handcuffs being escorted out of his office flashed across the screen. "It's all over every news station," Tiffany sadly told Mya. Mya focused in on the words flashing across the bottom of the screen. "Detroit King Pin Arrested on Drug Charges and faces up to life in prison." Mya didn't realize she was holding her breath until she began to feel dizzy. Tiffany jumped out Mya's way as she grabbed her purse and bolted for the door. At that moment, Mya was glad no one knew that her and King were separated but their mothers. Mya was a few blocks away from her job when it dawned on her that she had no idea where she was headed. She didn't have a clue who King's lawyer was because he kept Mya in the dark about his street life in order to protect her. Mya pulled over to the side off the road and frantically grabbed her phone from her purse and dialed the first person who came to her mind. Praying Don picked up, Mya called him back to back for five minutes straight before finally giving up. She said a silent prayer for King and Don because her gut told her they were going to need it. Mya anxiously snatched her phone off her lap when it began to ring hoping it was someone calling with news about King. She angrily smashed the decline call button when James' number flashed across the screen. Whatever her and James had was now over. King needed her. Making a mental note to have her number changed, Mya made a quick U-turn in the middle of the street and headed to King's mother's house. Mya tried her best to remain calm when she saw the worried look on Ms. Brenda's face when she opened the door and let Mya in. Ms. Brenda led Mya into the kitchen where she was keeping herself busy baking her famous apple pies that King loved so much. Mya could feel the tension in the air and was afraid to ask the dreaded question out of fear of what the answer would be. Mya finally broke the silence after a few minutes. "Is it that bad Mama Brenda?" Mya whispered. Ms. Brenda turned and looked Mya in the eyes. Although King and

Mya were separated Ms. Brenda knew Mya truly loved her son. She walked over to Mya and pulled her in for a hug. "I don't know baby! I'm waiting to hear from his lawyer now. King prepared himself just in case this day every came. He is a strong man; we just have to be strong for him right now." Ms. Brenda's words soothed Mya's heart and mind. Mya helped Ms. Brenda around the kitchen while they mentally prepared themselves for the battle ahead of them. Mya decided to stay a few nights over Ms. Brenda's house. They would both need each other support emotionally, physically, and mentally over the next few days. Mya dashed home and flew through her house like a tornado. She threw a few outfits, pajamas, a toothbrush, and her phone charger in her overnight bag and was back out the door in less than ten minutes. On the way back to Ms. Brenda's house Mya stopped by the house she once shared with King. A flood of memories washed over her the minute she pulled into the driveway. Mya scolded herself. Now wasn't the time to get emotional. She quickly wiped away her tears, jumped out the car and rushed onto the porch. Mya prayed her keys still worked as she stuck her key into the lock. She breathed a loud sigh of relief at the sound of the lock clicking open. Pushing the door open, Mya walked into the house and looked around. She was happy that everything was still the exact way she left it. Mya put her heart into decorating her and King's first home and realized how much she missed being there. She dashed up the stairs and giggled at the messy bedroom. Clothes were thrown all over the place and the bed looked like it hadn't been made up in days. Mya walked into their private bathroom and dropped down to her knees beside the tub. She tapped the cold marble tub along the side in several different spots until one tile popped open. The space was just big enough for Mya to stick her hand in. She wiggled her fingers around inside until they brushed against what she was looking for. Mya pressed down on the button inside and stood up while the marble tub slid back revealing the floor safe King had installed. King showed Mya where the safe was just in case anything ever happened to him. King changed the combination to the safe once per month as a precaution. Mya was disappointed when she punched in the last combination, she remembered which was King's mother's birthday and it didn't work. After trying her birthday, King's birthday, and their wedding anniversary Mya was ready to give up. She slammed her hand against the floor in frustration and began to sob. "Think Mya," she scolded herself. Mya suddenly remembered the lottery list of numbers King played every day faithfully. She ran over to the nightstand on King's side of the bed and yanked the top drawer open. Not caring about the mess, she was making, Mya dumped the entire drawer out on the bed. She ruffled through the papers until she found a thick stack of old lottery tickets. She quickly scanned the tickets and grabbed the one that stood out to her the most. The number on the ticket was a combination of the first two digits of her birthday and the last two numbers of their anniversary. Mya went back into the bathroom and slowly punched the number into the keypad on the safe. She squealed in delight when the safe popped open. Mya gasped when she saw the large stacks of money neatly tucked inside. She ran over to the closet and grabbed out King's oversized traveling luggage. Mya quickly piled the money into the suitcase before carefully concealing the safe back under the tub. It took Mya fifteen minutes to drag the heavy luggage down the stairs and load it into the car. Mya needed to do one more thing before leaving the house. She walked into the garage and popped the trunk on King's custom BMW. Mya once again tapped on a few panels in the trunk until one popped open. Mya nervously waited while a secret panel slid from under the side of the car. King had no idea Mya even knew about this stash spot. She only discovered it after waking up in the middle of the night to find King not in bed with her. After searching the house Mya was just about to pick up her phone and call him when she heard a noise coming from inside the garage. Mya caught a glimpse of King putting the car back together just before she ducked back inside. Mya slipped back upstairs and pretended to be sleep when King eased back in the bed a few minutes later. She never mentioned anything to King about what she saw that night and now as she stared down at the contents hidden in the panel, she understood why King didn't want her to know anything about it. Mya wasn't street smart, but she wasn't naive either. She knew the number of drugs she was looking at could send King to prison for a very long time. Mya was glad she decided to wear her oversized purse today because it came in handy. After stuffing the bricks of cocaine inside her purse, Mya pushed the button to conceal the panel back and closed the trunk back down. She walked through the house one last time to make sure she hadn't missed anything. Once she was satisfied, Mya cut the alarm on the house before jumping in her car and pulling off. She made sure she did the speed limit the whole way to her job. She knew it was too risky to keep the drugs at her or Ms. Brenda's house. Mya decided the best place to stash them was at her job. King wasn't the only one with secret stash spots. Mya's mother taught her at an early age to always prepare for a rainy day. As a perk, Mya's job offered free onsite safe deposit boxes to all of their financial consultants. From the day she was hired, Mya would stash a little money out of every paycheck into her safe deposit box at her job. After being betrayed by King and Star, Mya convinced her assistant Tiffany to switch safe deposit boxes with her just in case King started snooping around. Mya already had a separate bank account from King, but she wanted to take extra measures to make sure her future was secure. She didn't think King would try to do her dirty by coming after her assets if they were to divorce but Mya was not about to take any chances. Mya walked through the huge glass doors and nodded at the security guard James on duty. "Late night?" James casually asked when Mya strolled past him. Mya turned and smiled at him. "Actually, I left something upstairs in my office. I'll be back down shortly." Mya made sure to make her plump ass bounce and jiggle as she walked away to distract him. She stepped on the elevator and glanced at her watch, noticing it was nearly seven in the evening. The building was pretty much empty because everyone had already gone home for the day. Mya opened her safe deposit box that still read Tiffany's name and pulled out two large stacks of money. She pushed the rest of the money all the way to the back and stuffed the drugs from her purse inside. After placing the two stacks back inside and making sure the drugs was concealed, Mya locked the box. She calmly waved bye to James and walked to her car feeling a thousand pounds lighter now that she had the drugs put up in a safe place. "The things a woman will do for her man," Mya mumbled to herself.

Chapter 8

KING

King nervously paced back and forth in the small jail cell anxiously waiting to get his one phone call. He knew the Feds were only trying to stall time while they secured the search warrant for his home. King cringed thinking about the drugs stashed in the trunk of his car in the garage at his home. Although the drugs were stashed in a secret compartment of the car, King knew once the K-9's picked up the scent of drugs, the Feds would break his car down like a Lego to find them. He rarely kept drugs at home, and one of the few times he did, this shit happened. It was the first of the month which meant it was time for King to re-up all his spots. King didn't like to pull up to his spots in broad daylight, so he planned to drop off the drugs at nightfall but was arrested at his office before he got the chance to do so. While King was being processed in, he caught a glimpse of Don in handcuffs in the next room. The only person left King knew he could depend on was his number one lieutenant, Rico. Rico reminded King of a younger version on himself. Outside of Don he was the only one King trusted. Rico was smart and quick on his feet and King knew Rico would be able to read between the lines and understand what King needed him to do. King had to get rid of those drugs from his house ASAP. Every time an officer walked past his cell King prayed, they were coming to retrieve him for his one phone call. King knew his mother and Mya were worried sick about him, but he tried to prepare them as best he could for this day. He just hated Mya and he were on such bad terms when this happened. He could only hope she would put their differences to the side and stand by him during the time he needed her the most. King's name was finally called after being in the musty, stale, cramped cell jail for over five hours. Instead of being escorted to the phone, King was escorted to the interrogation room. "Well if it isn't the famous King," a tall, bald head, detective who resembled Morris Chestnut chuckled when King walked into the room. "My name is Detective James and I'm the lead detective on your case."

King remained silent and took a seat across from the detective. He planned to get any information he could from the detective before lawyering up. "Not in the talking mood, huh?" Detective James smirked. King could tell from the detective's cocky demeanor he had something on King. Tired of the back and forth games, King asked to speak with his lawyer. Detective James smiled and slid a white piece of paper across the table in front of King. "Sure, no problem," he smirked. "But make sure you inform him of this." King's heart fluttered as his eyes scanned the paper. Just as he thought, the Feds were procrastinating on giving him one call because they were trying to secure their search warrant for his home first. The detectives purposely took their time processing him through the system because they knew if King made a phone call, he would be able to tip someone off and destroy any evidence the police could find. "Officers are going through your home with a fine-tooth comb as we speak," Detective James smirked as he stood to leave. King kept a poker face in front of the detective, but his mind was racing a million miles per minute on the way back to his cell. There was no way King could justify having four kilos of cocaine concealed in a stash spot within his car. King and Don's lawyer Richard was the best in the city, but it would take God himself to get King out of this mess. If the

Feds found the drugs hidden at his house, they would have grounds to freeze all his bank accounts. King quickly did the math on how much money he had stashed in other places. There was over three million dollars in two different account overseas in both him and his mother's name and half a million dollars stashed inside a secret safe inside him and Mya's house. With everything going on the last few months. King never got around to giving Mya the new combination to the safe and there was no way possible Mya would be able to figure it out. King never used the same password twice and changed it once per month. After using his, Mya's, and his mother's birthday, King began using his favorite lottery numbers. He highly doubted if Mya would even remember him showing her the safe and even if she did there was no way possible, she would be able to figure out the last code he used. King dropped his head in defeat. He wasn't sure if he would even be given a bond and if he was lucky enough to get one it would be extremely high. King slammed his fist against the wall and stared unfazed at the blood dripping down his knuckles. He couldn't be mad at anyone but himself.

Chapter 9
DETECTIVE JAMES

"Fuck!" Detective James yelled, knocking the expensive crystal vase off the glass table sitting in the middle of King and Mya's living room. The officers in the room glanced in his direction and quickly went back to searching the house hoping to find something to satisfy the detective. Everyone knew how bad Detective James' temper was and nobody wanted to be his next victim. His team had kicked in the front door of King's mini mansion with a search warrant in hand over three hours ago and still hadn't found anything. No guns or drugs, and besides a couple of crumbled up hundred-dollar bills on the dresser, no money. NOTHING! King tried his best to seem unfazed earlier in the interrogation room, but Detective James could see the fear in King's eyes. As a detective for over twenty years he witnessed that same look on the face of many men. It was the look of a man who knew he was fucked and was possibly going to prison for a long time. "There has to be something here. Find it," he barked at the officers in the room. As the officers scurried around the house, Detective James stepped outside on the front porch for a breath of fresh air. Pulling a pack of Newport cigarettes from his pocket he sat on the porch made from different exotic stones and looked around. Detective James grimaced as he took in the scenario around him. King was living the type of life Detective James could only dream about. King was rich, with a beautiful home and a fleet of luxury cars that belonged on the cover of a magazine while he was barely surviving and living check to check. Not to mention Mya, King's beautiful wife. Detective James could feel the bulge in his pants start to rise as he thought about the thick, chocolate beauty he met a two months ago while attending a financial investment class. When one of his colleagues told him about the financial advisor who could help him invest his retirement savings and turn it into a large amount of cash Detective James jumped at the chance. After being forced to give his ex-wife over half of his savings when they divorced three years ago, Detective

James knew unless he found a way to invest the little money left in his bank account, he would never be able to retire. Two Months Ago Detective James was shocked when Mya walked into the conference room that was set up like a class and introduced herself as the instructor. She looked young enough to be his daughter. Her beauty and intelligence captivated him from the moment he laid eyes on her. He loved the way her light brown eyes lit up every time she smiled or laughed. Detective James would often make up reasons to stay after class and ask Mya any kind of questions he could think of just to get a whiff of her sweet vanilla scent. Detective James became more infatuated with Mya each time he saw her. Within three months Mya's investment advice had tripled his savings. For the first time in years he had hopes of being able to retire and living comfortably. It took some persuasion, but Detective James convinced Mya to join him for a drink after class to celebrate their success. He could tell something was going on with Mya because her eyes no longer sparkled like they used to. He was praying whatever man in her life had slipped up giving him an opportunity to slip in. They walked two blocks over to a dimly lit wine café. Mya was immediately impressed by the restaurant's romantic décor the minute they walked through the door. Each table sat in the middle of six-inch-high, black and gold plush leather booths which provided an intimate and private area for each guest. Crystal chandeliers hung directly over each table draped in gold embroidered tablecloths that hung down to the floor further enhancing the romantic atmosphere. Detective James chose a quiet booth toward the back of the café. He enjoyed the view of Mya's plump ass bouncing and jiggling under the tight mini skirt that hugged her frame as they made their way over to the table. The two made small talk while they looked over the menu and waited on the waitress to come take their order. They decided on a bottle of Chardonnay with a platter of sushi. Mya was thrilled when the bubbly waitress informed them, they were just in time for the nightly, live, erotic poetry reading. Mya loved poetry and erotic urban books. Zane was one of her favorite authors. She looked over at Detective James and smiled. "How did you know I liked poetry?" she asked. "I saw you reading a poetry book the other day in class," he answered, with a sly smirk on his face. Mya blushed at his response. This was her first time being out with a man since her and King separated, and she had to admit it was nice enjoying the company of a man again. The two enjoyed their wine and sushi while they waited on the show to start. Mya loosened up after her second glass of wine and admitted to Detective James she was married but separated. He could see the pain in her eyes while she discussed her husband's infidelities and hoped she would one day let him make her pain go away. When the lights dimmed, and the first poet walked out on stage he pulled Mya into his arms. He fought to keep his composure at the feel of Mya's soft ass snuggled up against him. He could feel her body relax as he massaged her neck and shoulders through the sexy lace blouse she was wearing. Can I drink you Can I taste you Can I lick you Can I sip you Not part of you All of you The poet's sultry voice filled the air. The crowd was mesmerized as she took the microphone between her hands and began to caress it back and forth. Your taste is so sweet Sweet like honey Detective James placed his hand on Mya's leg underneath the table and began caressing her thigh. When she let out a soft moan his hand began to explore further. He could feel the heat coming from between her legs as his fingers inched closer to her treasure box. He gently massaged her lower lips through the thin lace panties she was wearing while he nibbled on her neck. He could feel the moisture seeping through her thin panty material as his thumbs made circular motions around her clit. Tired of her panties being in the way he reached up and slid them down over her thick thighs, pleased when she slightly lifted her hips to assist him. After taking a quick glance around the café he was relieved when he noticed the few people in the restaurant were so into the poet no one was paying them any attention. He was glad he had chosen a booth all the way toward the back. Before Mya could protest, Detective James dipped his head underneath the long tablecloth and in between Mya legs. He quickly inhaled her sweet scent before devouring her. He placed a firm grip on her hips then dipped and swirled his tongue inside her neatly shaved kitty. Her juices tasted sweet like honey as they flowed from her body onto his lips. He took her pearl between his lips and softly sucked on it like a newborn baby. When he felt her legs begin to tremble, he inserted two fingers into her and began sucking harder. Mya wasn't sure if it was the wine, the erotic poems, or simply not being touched by a man in months that had her in pure ecstasy, but she loved every minute of it. She couldn't believe she was letting a man she barely knew, orally please her underneath a table in a public restaurant. It took everything in her not to scream out loud at the sensations Detective James was sending through her body. Can I drink you Can I taste you Can I lick you Can I sip you Not part of you All of you Mya threw her head back and let the poet's sexy words and Detective James' powerful tongue bring her to the best orgasm of her life. Her body tingled from head to toe. She tried to wiggle out of his grip but was too weak. Detective James savored each drop of

Mya's juices. He wanted to let her go but couldn't. He waited until her body stopped shivering and dove back in. Her pussy was a drug and he was addicted. He had never tasted something sweet and good in his life. He feasted on her goodies over the next hour while she sipped wine and enjoyed poetry, bringing her body to countless orgasms. Detective James didn't slide from under the table until the last poet left the stage. He licked his lips before taking a sip of wine and pulling out his wallet to take care of the bill. Mya felt like she was walking on air as they made their way out of the restaurant walking hand in hand. He winked at the waitress and slipped her a two-hundred-dollar tip for not interrupting them. "Maybe this single life won't be so bad," Mya giggled to herself. Over the next few weeks Detective James investigated criminal cases during the day and Mya's body at night. Although Mya wasn't ready to engage in intercourse with him just yet, she certainly didn't mind his head bobbing between her legs every chance she could get. The things he could do with his tongue were incredible. She pinched her nipples as she looked down at Detective James' bald head shining between her legs. Pushing her legs back far as they could go, he lightly blew down her ass crack before sliding his tongue back and forth across her juicy slit. He reached down and began to stroke himself while Mya rotated her hips to match his rhythm. Within minutes both of their bodies were rocking with orgasms. Detective James didn't care about having sex with Mya because he loved her. Long as she was good, he was good. To Mya, this was nothing more than a fling until she was ready to take King back. What she didn't know was Detective James had fallen in love with her and cutting him off wasn't going to be that easy. Everything was going great until Mya suddenly stopped accepting his phone calls. He left hundreds of voicemails on both her job and cellphone with no reply. It wasn't until he was assigned to King's case that he understood why. Imagine his surprise when going over King's file he stumbled across a picture of Mya with the word "wife" wrote across the bottom of the photo in bold red letters. Mya had stopped all communication with him around the exact time King was arrested. The thought of losing Mya to King enraged him. He was determined to do anything in his power to send King away for the rest of his life. Mya and his future depended on it.

Chapter 10

RICHARD
(KING AND DON'S LAWYER)

Richard tilted his rearview mirror to double check his appearance before getting out the car. He straightened his tie before grabbing his suitcase and heading into the court building. Richard made sure he used the back-security door assigned for attorneys only, to avoid the media. He didn't want to take the chance of having his face plastered all over the media as King and Don's lawyers. While King and Don may not have recognized who he was, Richard knew if Star found out she would surely expose him and ruin his entire plan. Today was King and Don's bail hearing and Richard wanted to ensure they both stayed behind bars. With Don out of the picture Star would be forced to realize how much she needed him. There was no way Star could afford to maintain the expensive lifestyle she was accustomed to living by herself and that would force her right back into Richard's arms and his bed. Richard walked into the courtroom and shook hands with a few other attorneys before taking a seat on the front row. King instructed Richard to contact his mother and Mya and inform them of his bail hearing. Richard made sure his secretary informed them of the wrong time, so he didn't run into Mya. If everything went according to plan the bail hearing would be over by the time her and Ms. Brenda arrived at court. Don's name was called first. Two officers escorted him out in an orange jump suit and shackles. Don didn't bother to look back and see who was in the courtroom because he knew nobody was there for him. Don was an only child and lost his mother to cancer three years ago. He never knew his father and refused to get close to any of his jump offs until he met Star. Don was tempted to call her the day he was arrested but decided against it. "Fuck her," he thought knowing his heart felt something completely different. Don stood in silence as the judge read off his list of charges including drug trafficking, drug manufacturing, drug distribution, and money laundering. After Richard weakly "argued" back and forth with the prosecutor on why Don wasn't a flight risk and why he should be given a bond, ultimately Don was denied bail. Richard breathed a deep sigh of relief as Don was escorted back to his jail cell. Don walked back to his cell feeling confused. "What the hell just happened?" he wondered. Don felt for some reason Richard hadn't argued his case for bail like he should have. Richard was normally more aggressive than he was today. Don just hoped Richard had some type of trick up his sleeve. King's name was called next. Unlike Don, King anxiously looked out into the courtroom to see who was there as he was escorted in. His heart dropped when he didn't see neither Mya nor his mother. King wasn't sure if Mya would be there but worried why his mother didn't make it. There was no way she would miss something so important. King leaned over and whispered to Richard "Did you call my mother and give her my court date and time?" Richard never looked up from the stack of papers he was nervously shuffling around. "Of course," he mumbled. Before King could respond the judge called the court to order. Standing stone faced, King listened as the judge read the laundry list of drug charges against him as well. King side eyed Richard as he briefly stated why King should be allowed out on bail. King was fuming as he stood next to Richard. He could have argued his case better himself. "Bail denied," the judge barked while slamming down his gavel. King glared at Richard as the bailiffs led him back to cell. He felt in his gut something was off and promised to get to the bottom of it.

Chapter 11

MYA

Mya and Ms. Brenda dashed into the courtroom and were shocked to look around and see it empty except for an elderly clerk who appeared to be packing up for lunch. "Excuse me ma'am," Mya walked up to her and politely said. "I'm here for husband's arraignment." The elderly clerk could see the worry in Mya's eyes and felt sympathy for her. Day after day she witnessed women like Mya worried and stressed out over some man's mess. She couldn't judge them because she was one of them many years ago. Thank God her husband Richard had changed his life around and was now one of the city's top lawyers. If only she could get him to keep his dick in his pants, she sadly thought. Her and Richard had been married for over thirty years. She had stuck by his side when he was fighting an embezzlement case, worked two jobs to help put him through law school and not to mention the countless affairs she endured. And what was the thanks she got? Her walking into her own home and finding some young, high yellow, tramp straddled across Richard's face while he slurped and licked on her pussy like a lollipop. She was so shocked she couldn't do anything but stand there and cry while she watched the woman's body shake from the orgasm HER husband's tongue was giving her. The same tongue that hadn't touched his own wife's kitty in years. Even worse, Richard confessed his love for his mistress right there in front of her and gave her a choice "accept it or leave." Because she had been the only one working while Richard attended law school, she had taken out all his school loans in her name, which meant she was deep in debt. There was no way she would be able to survive off the small salary she made working at the courthouse. So, she stayed. She slept on the couch that night and listened to her husband make love to another woman all night in the bed they once shared; while her mind and heart filled with rage, and a plan for revenge. The sound of Mya's nails anxiously tapping against the clerk's desk snapped the clerk back to reality. Sighing, she sat her lunch bag down and clicked on her computer. Hopefully she could get the young lady some information quickly and still get to the breakroom in enough time to catch the beginning of her favorite soap opera. Mya gave the woman King's information and nervously chewed on her bottom lip while she waited on some type of information. "His hearing was this morning sweetie," the clerk informed Mya and Ms. Brenda. They both gasped in shock. That couldn't possibly be right, Mya thought. She specifically remembered King's lawyer telling her the hearing was at one this afternoon. Ms. Brenda looked between the clerk and Mya in disbelief. She also remembered hearing the lawyer inform Mya of King's hearing time because Mya had spoken to him on speaker phone while the two of them were out grabbing a bite to eat. Seeing how upset Mya was becoming Ms. Brenda stepped in and kindly asked the clerk if King was given a bond. She knew the answer to her question before the elderly lady could even respond by the sudden sadness in her eyes. Neither King nor Don were granted a bond at their hearing. Tears trickled down Mya's face and she dropped her head in defeat. "Don't worry baby. Everything is going to be okay," Ms. Brenda said while rubbing Mya's back, unsure of who she was trying to convince more, herself or Mya. King laid across his bunk in deep thought. His gut told him something wasn't right. With Richard being one of the top lawyers in the city and the weak evidence the prosecutor had against King and Don, he should have been able to get them both out on bond, but he didn't. King went over several possibilities in his head but couldn't come up with one logical reason Richard would benefit from him and Don staying in jail. King's thoughts drifted to Mya and he smiled. His stomach was in knots during his entire bail hearing listening to the evidence against him. He was just waiting on the moment the cocaine stashed from inside his car was brought into the courtroom as evidence. When this never happened, King knew somehow Mya had managed to get rid of the drugs and money before the police arrived. King wasn't sure how she pulled it off and could only pray Mya was smart enough not to take anything back to her or his mother's house because more than likely their house would be searched next. Once he finally got out of here, King vowed to make things right with Mya no matter how long it took. He owed her his love and loyalty for life. King swung his legs over the bunk and began doing sit ups to take his mind off everything going on. "99! 100!" Just as

King reached his one-hundredth push up, a folded piece of paper slid under his cell. King stood up and walked cautiously toward the folded-up note. After cautiously looked around outside his cell, he discreetly bent down and picked it up. Carefully unfolding the letter, King slowly read the one line wrote in big, bold letters across the middle of the paper. "We Have an Enemy Among Us!" The message was from Don. King and Don were best friends for years, King could identify Don's handwriting anywhere. It wasn't hard for King to read between the lines and understand Don's message loud and clear. Don was currently sitting somewhere in the same county jail as King and thinking the same thing, Richard was a snake that needed to be cut out the grass. But first they had to find a way to get out of this mess.

Chapter 12

STAR

Star sat inside the food court at the mall, rubbing her slightly protruding belly as she enjoyed the perfectly seasoned chicken stir fry. She was glad she decided to get out the house for a while. Unemployed, and no longer friends with Mya, her days were spent sulking around the house with nothing to do. The only thing that brought Star any form of joy was the precious baby she would soon be bringing into the world. Since the day Star heard her child's heartbeat for the first time, she would sit and rub her stomach for hours a day, singing and talking to her baby. While she wasn't proud of being pregnant and not knowing if the father was King or Don, she didn't regret the life growing inside of her. Even if she had to do it alone, Star promised herself, and her child, that she would be the best mother possible. Star finished the last of her food while deciding what store to begin shopping at. She didn't know if she was having a boy or girl yet but figured she could buy some things in neutral or pastel colors. Her excitement kicked in the minute she walked into Children's Palace. Star cooed over all the cute little outfits in different sizes and colors. When a salesgirl came over and asked Star if she had decided on a theme for her baby room yet, Star looked at her in confusion. "This must be your first one?" the salesgirl laughed. "Come with me!" Sitting Star down in front of a guest computer, the salesgirl clicked on a link on the computer screen that read "Baby Themes." Pointing to the screen she explained to Star most parents pick out a baby theme to decorate their child's room in. "Common themes are Mickey Mouse and Winnie the Pooh," she told Star. Star was becoming overwhelmed looking at all the different room designs. "How far are you?" the bubbly salesgirl asked. "Four months," Star happily told her. "No worries. You have plenty of time to decide on a theme for your baby. I'm sure you have plenty of family and friends to help you." The sudden look of sadness that washed over Star's face made the clerk instantly regret saying those words. It was apparent Star was going through this pregnancy alone. Feeling the sudden awkwardness, the salesclerk excused herself to go help another customer. "Let me know if you need anything," she called out over her shoulder while quickly walking away. Star sat at the computer a little longer clicking through the different pictures. When suddenly it hit her. "Unicorns. My baby's theme will be unicorns," she excitedly told herself. Unicorns represented something unique, beautiful and mysterious. "Yes, that's it," she happily sang out loud. Flagging the salesgirl down Star inquired about any unicorn items in the store. Relieved that she hadn't said anything to make Star report her to the store manager, the salesgirl eagerly walked Star over to the aisle filled with different animal merchandise. By the time Star walked out the store, her arms were filled with bags full of items for her baby. If she continued shopping like this, Star would have no other choice but to find a job after she delivered her baby. She was done with the whole "Using what you got, to get what you need." Star was going to be someone's mother soon and it was time she started acting like it. Pulling into her driveway, Star rushed to get all the bags in the house, ready to get into something comfortable and sit in front of her television with a huge bowl of chocolate chip ice cream. Star struggled to unlock the door as she balanced all the bags in both hands. A foul odor attacked her nose the minute she stepped into the house. Star walked further into the house while trying to remember what she could have placed in the garbage with such a foul smell. The feel of something mushy under her foot caused Star to look down. She screamed out in horror when she realized what the horrible smell traveling throughout her house was. Dead rats were scattered everywhere throughout her living room leaking blood on her beautiful white carpet. The word Slut was written across her white couch in what appeared to be blood. Star slowly backed out of the house in shock and scared for her life. Star jumped back in her car and rushed to the police station. Pulling into the police station parking lot, Star parked in the first available spot she saw not caring if she was parking illegal or not. Dashing into the building, she pushed past several people who were waiting to make a report. Ignoring their mumbles, she walked right up to the desk and asked to speak with someone immediately. Several other officers rushed into the lobby after hearing all the commotion. After calming Star down she was asked to have a seat and a detective would be out to see how soon. Turning around she locked eyes with Mya and King's mother. Mya's mouth dropped open in shock when her eyes wondered down to Star's round belly. "You Bitch," Mya screamed. Before she could take off in Star's direction Ms. Brenda grabbed her by the arm. "King is already locked up. We can't have you locked up with him. This is not the time or place," she scolded Mya, while wanting to take Star outside herself and give her an old school beating. Star avoided Mya's angry glare and the stares of the nosy bystanders as she took a seat in the corner and waited for a detective to come out and see her. What the hell was Mya and Ms. Brenda doing in the police station anyway. She didn't want Mya to find out this way, but right now she had more important things to worry about. Protecting her and her unborn baby's life was her number one priority. Everyone was so distracted by their own thoughts; nobody noticed the dark figure in the shadows watching their every move.

Chapter 13

MYA

Mya was beyond heartbroken as she got in her car after leaving the police station. After waiting over an hour to speak with the detective on King's case her and Ms. Brenda discovered not only was King's next court date a whole month away, Star was possibly pregnant with King's baby. "This can't be happening," she cried. Mya was glad her and Ms. Brenda drove separate cars so she could be alone in her misery. If that was in fact King's baby their marriage was over. Mya could forgive him for cheating. After all, she felt like they were now even because she had slept with King's best friend. But there was no way in hell she would accept a baby her husband made with her best friend. The constant ringing of her cellphone began to annoy her. Grabbing her phone from her purse, Mya didn't bother to check the caller Id before answering it. "Hello???" Mya yelled into the phone. "Mya, baby I miss you," James whined into the phone. Mya sucked her teeth. She thought by now James would have gotten the message that what they had was over. Mya gritted her teeth as she listened to James beg and plead to see her. She didn't have time for this shit right now. "James listen. What happened between us was a mistake. It's over." Mya's harsh words stunned James. She had never spoken to him in such a manner. His body began to fill with rage. "You whore," he yelled through the phone. "You are scum just like your husband!" James yelled and immediately regretted his words once they left his mouth. "How do you know my husband?" Mya whispered in shock. James didn't respond. He simply hung up the phone. Mya sat behind the steering wheel in a daze. The hatred in James' voice gave her chills. The more she thought about things, the more she realized she didn't really know much about James at all. But she had an easy way to find out. Because James was one of her financial clients, her company would have a file on him containing all his personal information. Sending her assistant Tiffany, a quick text message asking her to pull James' file, Mya headed over to her office. She planned on paying Ms. Star a visit later, but first she had other things to get to the bottom of. Mya sat behind her desk and anxiously shifted through the papers in front of her. Her stomach filled with knots the more she read. Not only was James a police detective, he was the lead detective over all high-profile drug cases in the city, which meant he was the detective in charge of King's case. That would explain how he knew King. Mya was sleeping with the enemy and didn't even know it. "Damn," she muttered to herself in disbelief. Was she the reason King was sitting behind bars? How could she have been so careless and stupid? Mya had to find a way to fix this and fast. Calling King's lawyer, she impatiently waited for him to pick up the phone. When his voicemail finally picked up, Mya couldn't help but to think how familiar his voice sounded. Hanging up she called right back to listen to the recorded message again. Mya's cellphone made a loud thud noise when it slipped from her hands and bounced off the floor. "No. It couldn't be!" Mya gasped. Her brain was racing to keep up with all her thoughts. The voice Mya just listened to sounded exactly like the older man Star had brought to her and King's wedding. Mya tried her best to recall his name but came up blank. Star only dated rich men so it wouldn't be too farfetched to assume he was possibly a lawyer. But if that was the case why had King or Don not recognized him. There was only one way to find out if her suspicions were true. Mya grabbed her purse and raced out the door to Star's house.

****

Star was enjoying the soothing jazz music playing over the Boise stereo system throughout the house while she packed the last of her boxes. Even after having a professional company come in and paint and replace the carpet throughout her house, Star could still smell the foul odor of blood. She no longer felt safe in her own home and decided to move into a newly remodeled condo on the other side of town. There was no way she was going to stay in a house with her child where a crazy manic could pop up at any moment. Just as she was about to tape up the last box in the kitchen, Star's doorbell rung and caught her off guard. Not expecting any company, Star grabbed a steak knife out of one of the boxes she was packing and eased toward the front door. She was surprised when she looked out the peephole and saw Mya standing on the other side. She sat the knife down and cracked the door just enough to stick her head out. "We need to talk Star," Mya said pushing the door open and brushing past her. Star took a deep breath and closed the door. Making sure her cell phone was securely tucked into her back pocket she followed Mya into the living room. Star felt bad about the way she'd betrayed Mya, but she wasn't about to get into a physical altercation with her and risk losing her child. She would call the police in a heartbeat and have Mya arrested if she tried to get physical with her in any type of way. Star sat on the couch across from Mya and unconsciously rubbed her belly. When she noticed the look of disgust on Mya's face she instantly stopped. "Is King the father?" Mya asked just above a whisper. Star hesitated for a moment trying to think of the best way to answer Mya's question. She didn't want to lie to Mya and say no when there was a good possibility King was indeed the father. It would just complicate things down the line when Star had her baby. "Mya I'm sorry for everything I did to you. I was selfish and jealous of you when all you ever tried to be was a good friend to me. I regret a lot of the choices I made but unfortunately, I can't take any of them back. In my heart I'm praying Don is the father of my child, but yes there is a small possibility King could be the father as well." A million feelings flooded through

Mya's body. She began to feel lightheaded at the possibility of her husband having a baby by her ex best friend. Star jumped up and ran into the kitchen to wet a paper towel for Mya who looked like she was going to faint any minute. Rushing back into the living room, Star handed the wet napkin to Mya who instantly began to dab her face and neck. Then it hit her! "You Bitch," Mya screamed. "You manipulated me into killing my baby with my husband, now you might be pregnant by him." Before Star realized what was happening, Mya lunged toward her and grabbed a fistful of Star's hair. Knocking her back on the couch Mya used her weight to pin Star down. Whap! "Backstabbing bitch! Whap! Whap! I trusted you!" Mya screamed. Star didn't try to fight back. She used her arms to protect her stomach. "Mya please! I'm pregnant," Star sobbed. Mya released her grip on Star's hair and slowly climbed off her. Mya casually walked back over to her chair and sat down. She crossed her arms over her chest, satisfied looking over at Star busted lip and the huge knot forming on her forehead. Now we can discuss what I came here for," she smirked. "I need your help."

Chapter 14

STAR

Star listened intently to everything Mya was telling her. She had no idea King and Don were even in jail, although it was all over the news. Star barely watched television and when she did it was mostly her favorite shows recorded on her DVR. Star was even more shocked to learn Richard was possibly King's and Don lawyer. It was hard to believe neither King or Don would remember Richard from King and Mya's wedding, but after thinking about it, Star had kept Richard hidden in their suite most of the time. Star hadn't spoken to Richard in months. Once she found out she was pregnant Star blocked his number. She was determined not to go back to her old ways. Star knew how devious Richard could be. If he neglected to inform King and Don who he was, Star could guarantee Richard was up to no good. "Are you sure it's the same Richard?" Star asked in disbelief. "That's what we're about to find out," Mya stated. Mya grabbed her cellphone out her purse and pulled up the contact information for Richard stored in her phone. She began to read the telephone number out loud. "5-5-5- 1-3," Mya stopped when Star interrupted her "7-4," finishing the last two numbers of Richard's phone number. They stared at each other in silence for a few minutes. "That sick bastard," Mya screeched. The pieces of the puzzle were slowly falling together. Why Richard gave Mya and Ms. Brenda the wrong time for King's court date, and why he always had them deal with his secretary. Richard knew if Mya saw him, she would recognize him right away. Star cringed at the fact that she was probably the reason Don was sitting behind bars. Once again, her past decisions were hurting and affecting the people around her that she loved. "I have a plan," Star said. Mya didn't know what Star planned on doing but she hoped it worked out in their favor.

Chapter 15

RICHARD
(KING AND DON'S LAWYER)

A huge smile spread across Richard's face as he looked down at the vibrating phone on his desk. Star's name flashed across the screen. Although he had been waiting on this call for months Richard casually answered the phone like he didn't have a care in the world. "Helllllo?" "Hey Richard," Star cooed through the phone. The soft sound of Star's voice instantly caused Richard's manhood to rise as he pictured her juicy lips wrapped around his piece. "So, you finally miss Daddy?" Richard chuckled through the phone. Star rolled her eyes thankful that Richard couldn't see the look of disgust plastered on her face through the phone. This was going to be a lot harder than she thought, Star realized. "Of course, I missed you Daddy," Star purred. After making small talk for a few minutes, Star and Richard made plans to have dinner later that evening. Star hung up with Richard and looked around at all the boxes scattered around her house. Everything was fully packed and ready for the movers who would be arriving in a few days. Fortunately, this would work out perfect for her plan. For the next few hours Star busied herself straightening up a few things. She ordered some takeout from Richard's favorite Thai restaurant down the street before jumping in the shower. After oiling her skin in Richard's favorite lavender scent, Star slipped on a silk nightie and was ready to put her plan into action...........

****

Richard hummed along to the oldies and goodies station on the fifteen-minute drive over to Star's house. He was so excited at the thought of finally being able to slide back into Star's warm and wet peach, he didn't notice the vehicle three cars behind following him. I knew it would just be a matter of time before she called me, he thought to himself. Richard knew Star's lifestyle was far too extravagant to afford alone. He gently stroked himself fantasizing about all the different positions he would put her in tonight. He was going to punish her for making him wait so long to be back between her legs. Pulling into Star's driveway, Richard turned off his headlights and grabbed the bottle of whiskey off the front seat before eagerly jumping out his car. He rang the doorbell and tapped his foot impatiently against the porch while he waited for Star to open the door. His mouth dropped open in surprise when she swung the door open a few seconds later. Her round baby bump stuck out underneath the sheer nightgown that clung to her body. "Don't worry it's not yours," Star smirked before moving to the side and letting him in. Richard was speechless as he walked into the house. Jealousy and rage filled his body at the thought of another man spilling his seeds inside Star. Richard knew it had to be Don's baby and he would stop at nothing to keep him locked up for the rest of his life. Star could sense Richard's anger, but she really didn't care. Standing across the room looking at him, Star felt disgusted with herself. How could she have belittled herself for years over this man? The more she looked at him she realized there was nothing attractive about him but his money. Fighting the urge to throw him out her house Star put on a fake smile. "I know this is a bit of a surprise to you," she said while seductively walking toward him. "But I miss you." Star swept her hair to one side of her head, purposely using her twenty-four inches of bone straight Brazilian weave to push one of the straps of her nightgown off her shoulders. The sight of Star's hardened nipples poking through the thin fabric made Richard instantly forget about her pregnancy. Star pushed Richard down on the couch and straddled her body across his lap. No longer able to contain himself Richard yanked Star's nightgown over her head. He marveled at the thickness of her body. Her pregnancy made her perky titties fuller and gave her hips southern spread. Star moaned as Richard took one of her breasts into his mouth and began to gently suck on her nipples. Picking her up and laying her back on the couch Richard placed his head between her legs and inhaled her sweet scent that he missed so much. While he did have a wife at home Richard had no desire to have sex with her at all. The only reason he was even still married to her was because he refused to give her half of everything he worked for even if she was there for him from the beginning. Being married over thirty years Richard's wife had let herself go and Richard no longer found her attractive. She was boring in bed and that was why Richard had started cheating on her in the first place. What type of wife refused to orally please her husband? The day Richard met Star he instantly fell in love. He was always attracted to younger girls because they were easier to manipulate. He had molded Star into the perfect mistress and refused to lose her to anybody. He would just have to figure out a way to get rid of that bastard child once she had him. Placing Star's leg on his shoulders Richard lightly flicked his tongue across her clit before slurping it completely in his mouth. Placing one finger deep inside her Richard began to finger Star's G-spot as her body shook. This wasn't a part of Star's plan, but her body desperately needed a release. The last time she had sex was with King and that was months ago. Feeling her orgasm build, Star grabbed the back of Richard's head and pushed his face further in her wetness. She grinded her hips against his lips as her juices flowed from her body. When Richard continued to devour her, Star spread her legs to give him better access. She was going to get every orgasm she could out the deal because she didn't know when another man would be between her legs. Richard finally came up for air after Star's fourth explosion. Licking her juices off his lips he stripped out of his clothes ready to feel her tight, wet kitty. He got excited just thinking about his piece being in the same space as Don's baby. "Wait," Star screeched sliding from underneath Richard just as he was about to push his hard erection into her. She had no plans of letting him stick his dirty dick anywhere near her unborn baby. "We need to talk." Richard looked at Star like she had grown two heads. Holding his throbbing dick in his hands he yelled "Now?" When Star crossed her arms over her chest Richard knew she wasn't going to budge. Sitting back on the couch he stroked himself while admiring her body. Walking over to where Richard had sat down the whiskey, she poured him a drink and handed it to him. "I'm losing my condo Richard; I need money to survive. Don't you see all the boxes?" For the first time since walking into the house, Richard looked around and noticed most of her things were packed. He was thrilled to know his plan had worked. Star needed him. Reaching down and grabbing his pants, Richard pulled out his checkbook. "No worries," he smirked. Richard was one of the top lawyers in the city. A person needed at least five thousand dollars just to consult with him. He had more than enough money to live comfortably and take care of one or two mistresses for the rest of his life. Writing Star a check for fifty thousand dollars, Richard signed it and handed it over to her. Star's eyes widened when she looked at the amount of the check. She didn't expect Richard to be so generous. She was only hoping for enough money to be able to pay her bills up at her new place until she delivered her baby. Star planned to find a job after she had her baby. "Let me go freshen up," Star seductively said. Richard gave Star a hard smack on the ass when she dashed by him. "Hurry up," he barked. "We are waiting on you," he laughed while stroking himself. Star went into her bedroom and safely tucked the check away. Grabbing her cellphone, she casually strolled back into the living room. "Come get on your knees and show Daddy how much you appreciate him." Star almost gagged at the thought. She sat on Richard's lap and hit the unlock button on her cellphone. Star already had the videos she wanted to play saved and ready to play. When the sounds of lovemaking began to play on the phone Richard smiled. "I see you in the mood to be naughty tonight, huh?" Richard asked while trying to slide his hands between Star's legs. When Star shoved the phone closer to his face Richard froze. On the screen was Star propped up on his desk spread eagle with Richard's mouth full of her pussy. Star sat across from Richard admiring his salt and pepper beard as he glanced over her resume. Star seductively crossed her legs causing the dress she wore to creep up her thighs, revealing she wore no panties underneath. After glancing over her resume and seeing Star had no experience Richard cut right to the chase. He kept his focus on Star's perky breast while asking, "You have no experience, why should we hire you?" Star stood up and smirked while walking over to the door and locking it. She slid her dress over her head and stood directly in front of Richard. "I have a lot of things I'm experienced at," she said, licking her lips. Star thought the old man was about to have a heart attack as beads of sweat rolled down his face. He loosened his tie as Star pushed some papers off his desk and perched herself on top of it. She spun around and spread her legs making sure her neatly shaved peach was within inches of Richard's face. Star gently sucked on her index finger and began massaging her clit. At the age of sixty Richard had not seen a young pretty pussy in years and his tongue hung out of his mouth at the beautiful sight. Before he knew it, Richard found himself face first between Star's thick legs. Richard was a playboy back in his day and by the way Star was thrashing around on his desk, he had not lost his touch. After Star came twice Richard bent her over his desk and plunged into her so hard the desk almost fell over. Star's tightness and warmth was sending him over the edge with each stroke. He panted and grunted as he gripped Star's waist and delivered powerful strokes. When Star felt herself about to cum again, she buried her head in some papers to keep from screaming out. Damn this old man good, she thought. Two orgasms later and Richard was in love. By the time Star left Richard's office, she had secured her job as his mistress instead of his receptionist. "You recorded us," Richard yelled, pushing Star off him. Star laughed at his discomfort. When she originally decided to record her and Richard's first sex act it was for "just in case" reasons. She had no idea that reason would be to help get the love of her life out of jail. "Oh, there is more," Star smirked. Pushing play on the next video, Richard looked like he was about to faint when he heard his voice offering Star to one of his co-workers for the night in exchange for a promotion. Making sure she was out of Richard's reach Star tilted her phone to give him a clear view of the next video. Star was bent over Richard's boss desk while he plunged in and out of her with a handful of her hair grasped tightly in his hand. "Now how would this look for your firm Richard, if this video got out?" she giggled. A bunch of old dirty LAWYERS passing around a seventeen-year-old for their sexual pleasure. "Se-Se-venteen!" Richard stuttered. "You told me you were eighteen when we met." Star laughed in his face.

"Well you certainly didn't ask for any ID, now did you?" Star saw the look in Richard's eyes and reached for her television remote, quickly hitting the power button. A clear image of them popped up on the screen. Star waved at the television to show Richard every move they made was being recorded. Star lived a dangerous life and made sure to install cameras all around any house she lived in. "What the fuck do you want bitch?" Richard snarled. "Now is that any way to talk to a lady?" Star taunted. "You have exactly one week to have King and Don released from jail or I will expose you and your entire law firm. You see what happened to R. Kelly didn't you? The public don't take kindly to child molesters," Star smirked. If looks could kill Star would have been dead on the spot. "How did you know I was King and Don's lawyer?" Richard thought he covered all his bases by avoiding Mya and all the television cameras covering King and Don's case but somehow his secret still got out. "It doesn't matter how I found out!" Star snapped. "What matters is you were willing to send two men who trusted you as their lawyer to prison over pussy. Now you have one week to fix the mess you created or I'm taking these videos to the media and the board of ethics." Richard began to throw on his clothes. By the look on Star's face he knew she wasn't playing. If those videos got out, they would not only ruin his career but his entire law firm also. At the demand of Richard, Star had slept with every senior partner in the firm. Terrified at possibly being the cause of a lot of ruined careers, Richard had to get King and Don released from jail ASAP. Sitting across the street from Star's house, behind the dark tinted windows of the rental car for over an hour debating on what to do, they were just about to pull off when Richard came dashing out the house. The look on his face was mixed with anger and fear. They watched stunned as Star stood in the doorway with a smirk on her face, watching Richard back his car out the driveway at a high rate of speed. "Star was PREGNANT," they said out loud in a daze. That must be why Richard was so upset when he left. Star must have called him over to give him the news. Hurriedly pulling off, they knew exactly what they had to do.

Chapter 16

KING AND DON

"All rise!" the bailiff yelled through the courtroom. The courtroom was packed. Mya, Star, Ms. Brenda, and Mya's mother sat on the front row of the courtroom, while everyone from the neighborhood packed the rows behind them. They were all there to show their support for King and Don at the emergency hearing that had been called. Mya and Star weren't back on good terms, but they were able to put their differences to the side to help King and Don. After someone "mysteriously" sent information to the judge that the informant from King and Don's case, whose information the entire case was built on, turned out to be related to one of the agents working on the case, Richard was able to get the judge to call an emergency hearing hoping to get the case thrown out and King and Don released immediately. His career depended on it. When King and Don were escorted into the courtroom Mya's heartbeat sped up. It had been nearly four months since she laid eyes on her husband and she missed him something terrible. Even in the orange jumpsuit and shackles his demeanor still screamed power. When King and Mya locked eyes, no words needed to be said. After everything that just went through, their bond was unbreakable, and they both knew they would do whatever was needed to make their marriage work. Star tried her best not to make eye contact with Don, but they happened to look each other's way at the same time. Whether Don wanted to admit it or not he was still in love with Star. Everyone in the courtroom held their breath as the judge disappointingly looked over his glasses at the paperwork in front of him. Richard sat in between King and Don with sweat pouring down his forehead. He didn't know how much they knew about his shady behavior, but he could tell from their body language they knew something. Neither man had spoken one word to him since being escorted into the courtroom. The only sound that could be heard throughout the courtroom was the shuffling of paperwork by the judge. King watched the judge in nervous anticipation. When King called his mother the other day and she told him he would be coming home soon, King wasn't quite sure what to expect. He had been sitting in the small cell for months and was slowly losing hope of getting out anytime soon. His mother's voice had so much confidence in it, King wondered what she had up her sleeve, but wouldn't dare ask her any questions over the jail's hot ass phone where everything was being recorded. He would just have to wait it out while praying for the best and preparing for the worst. When Richard paid King and Don an unannounced visit that morning to announce some important information had surfaced that could get them out, King knew something was up right away. Richard could not look King or Don in the eyes as he nervously shuffled around papers their entire visit. Not to mention the huge wet spots that had formed under the arms of his thousand-dollar silk shirt from the amount of sweat that poured from his body. The exact way he was sweating now sitting in the courtroom watching the judge with everyone else. Everyone's eyes shifted in the direction of the judge when he began to stack the papers in front of him into a neat pile. As much as the judge didn't want to, he would have no other choice but to dismiss the case against King and Don. The courtroom erupted in loud cheers when the judge announced King and Don were free to go. The judge banged his gavel several times to bring the court back to order. "Don't leave the state." The judge spat, as he angrily glared at King and Don. "This case is far from over." King and Don embraced in a long brotherly hug both men completely ignoring Richard standing near them. Mya ran up to King and nearly knocked him over when she jumped in his arms. Star was relieved King and Don would be released. She was proud that she was able to help them but still wasn't ready to face Don. She could only feel pity for Richard when King and Don found out he could have had them released months ago. Trying to hurry and slip out the courtroom Star grabbed her purse and stood to leave. The smile faded from both King and Don's face when Star stood to leave the courtroom. Staring at Star's huge round belly in shock they both were thinking the same thing. "Was Star carrying their baby?"

✶✶✶✶✶✶✶✶✶✶✶✶✶✶✶✶

For the last three days, Mya and King had been locked away inside the Presidential Suite of a lavish hotel equipped with everything from a California King sized bed with wall to ceiling mirrors, marble floors, a balcony with a beautiful city view and 5-star room service. King and Mya wanted to tune out everything and everybody and focus on just the two of them. King couldn't get enough of Mya. After enjoying passionate sex throughout the entire suite for two straight days. King and Mya spent the next day talking. King listened in awe as Mya told him about removing the drugs and money from the house and stashing it at her job before the police raided their home. King's heart filled with love, respect, and admiration for his wife. He owed Mya his life. If the police would have found those drugs, King would have been sent away to prison for a long time. He silently thanked God for bringing him and Mya back together and vowed to never do anything again that could tear them apart. When Mya finally got around to telling King about Detective James' connection to him and Don's case, King felt like Mya wasn't telling him everything. Something in his gut told him Detective James was more than just a person Mya gave financial advice to. King wanted to ask Mya if her and Detective James ever slept together but decided against it. After sleeping with Star and possibly getting her pregnant it wasn't much he could say even if she did. King was relieved to know Detective James retired from the police force once him and Don's case was dismissed. When it was King's turn to talk, he told Mya about the first night he slept with Star. Mya cringed listening to King go into details about that night. From getting drunk at the bar, to Star taking his keys and driving him and how they ended up having unprotected sex in his hotel room that night. When Mya asked King if it was a possibility of Star's child being his, King admitted it was a possibility. Tears flooded down Mya's face at the reality of hearing those words. That night King made love to Mya like it was the end of the world. He lost count of how may times he released his seeds deep into Mya. If Star was possibly going to have his child, he was determined that Mya would too. After hours of lovemaking King and Mya drifted off into a peaceful sleep both praying for one thing: King not to be the father of Star's child.

****

The sudden knocking on Star's door startled her. She was doing the final walk thru of her home making sure she hadn't forgotten anything. The movers had already come yesterday and moved all her furniture and clothes to her new house. She just needed to grab a few little odds and ends. "Who could that be," Star muttered, as she waddled to the door. She couldn't believe how big she had gotten almost overnight. With three more months left in her pregnancy, Star didn't know how much more weight she would be able to carry around. Peeking out the blinds, Star gasped when she saw Don standing on her porch. Creeping away from the door Star stumbled and had to catch her balance on the wall. "Open the door Star," Don called out. "I know you are in there." "Shit," Star cursed under her breath. Taking a deep breath, Star walked to the door and slowly pulled it open. Her stomach began to flutter looking into Don's beautiful eyes and deep dimples. "We need to talk!" Star didn't say anything as she trailed behind Don into the living room. Looking around Don noticed the house was completely empty besides two old chairs sitting in the middle of the room. "Moving?" he asked. Looking Don in the eyes, Star decided for the first time in her life to come clean about everything. Don and Star sat in the two chairs across from each other as she told him about her childhood growing up with a crackhead mother, her secret envy of Mya, her insecurities, how she met Richard and traded sex for money, how she seduced King into sleeping with her and how she blackmailed Richard into getting him and King released from jail. By the time she was finished, Star's face was flooded with tears and Don sat in the chair across from her in shock. For the first time in her life Star felt free. "I'm going to be honest. The baby I'm carrying could be yours or King's but I'm praying it's yours because I love you," Star whispered. This was all a lot for Don to take in at once. He loved Star but he couldn't imagine being with her if she gave birth to King's baby.But regardless of what happened between the two of them, Don would forever be grateful for what Star had done for him and King. Had she not blackmailed Richard into getting them released, there was no telling how long the two of them would have sat in jail for. Don stood and gave Star a light kiss on the forehead. He bent down and gently rubbed her belly. The were both shocked when they felt the baby give a powerful kick. "Wow," Star said in amazement. She felt like that was a sign that Don was the father of her baby. Don asked Star when her next doctor's appointment was and promised to be there. Because there was even a possibility, he was the father of Star's child, Don was going to be there for her the rest of her pregnancy. "Does this mean we can start over again?" Star asked hopefully. "Let's wait and talk about that once the baby is born and we get the DNA test done," Don said before walking out the door. Star closed the door behind

Don and leaned up against it full of excitement. Maybe she would have her "happily ever after" after all. Ready to get to her new place and get settled, Star started up the stairs to grab her purse from her old bedroom. She made it to the top if the stairs when she heard light taps on the front door. Thinking Don must have forgot something, Star rushed back down the stairs fast as she could. Not bothering to ask who it was, Star flung the door open. "What did you forg..." Before Star could finish her sentence, she was hit hard with something metal over the head and knocked out cold.

Chapter 17

STAR

Star's head felt like a load of heavy bricks as she slowly tried to lift it and look around. The room began to slowly come into focus under Star's heavy eyelids. Trying to move her arms, Star looked down and realized she was tied to one of the chairs sitting in the middle of her living room. The rag shoved in her mouth prevented her from screaming out loud. Star began to panic as she wildly thrashed around in the chair. She instantly froze when the sound of loud, evil laughter coming from behind her, suddenly filled the room, sending chills down her neck. Star tried to turn her head in the direction the laughter was coming from, but the ropes tied tightly around her wrists and ankles preventing her from doing so. When the shadowy figure came into view Star gasped in shock. "Surprised to see me?" Richard's wife snickered with a psychotic look in her eyes. Star instantly feared for her and her unborn baby's safety. "I hate young bitches like you," Richard's wife angrily ranted. "No respect for the next woman and her marriage. Do you think I am going to let you have a baby by my husband? When Richard's wife pulled a small black handgun from her back pocket Star's eyes grew wide with fear. Star had to find a way to let Richard's wife know the baby she was carrying did not belong to Richard. Whap… Richard's wife smashed the gun across Star's face, causing her head to snap to the side from the hard, swift blow. Star could feel her eye instantly begin to swell as blood trickled down her nose. "That's for fucking my husband in my bed," Richard's wife said, and spit in Star's face. Star thought back to the night Richard's wife walked in and caught her and Richard having sex in their home. Where Star should have been ashamed of being caught in another's woman's bed, she took pride in making Richard's wife suffer. A decision that would probably now cost her and her baby their lives. Star and Richard were in the middle of passionate sex in the same bed him and his wife shared for years. Richard's wife was supposed to be out to dinner with her friends until later that evening but returned home early not feeling well. Star's plump ass was damn near smothering Richard as she sat on his face enjoying how he sucked and licked on her clit. Just as Star was about to cum, Richard's wife came storming into the room. Richard tried to push Star off him, but her thick thighs were locked around his head. Star didn't give a fuck if Santa Claus walked in the room, her orgasm was too close to stop. Richards's wife stood in the doorway crying as Star grinded her hips on top of Richard's face, until her body was rocking from a powerful orgasm. She didn't release Richard's head until every drop was released from her body. Star rolled over on the bed to catch her breath while Richard sat up wiping Star's juices from his lips. "I didn't want you to find out this way, but I'm glad this is finally out in the open," he said. "This is my mistress, Star," Richard said, pointing over at Star who was still laying naked in the bed doing nothing to cover herself. "You either accept our relationship, or you can leave, but Star is here to stay," his voice boomed in an authoritative manner. Richards's wife backed out of the room, informing them she would be waiting downstairs until they finished. For the rest of the night Richard fucked Star in every position possible, while his wife sat downstairs on the couch and painfully listened. Star made sure her moans were loud enough to put on a show. When Richard's wife struck Star in the head with the gun again Star began to lose consciousness. Tears trickled down Star's face. Richard's wife roughly yanked the rag out of Star's mouth. "Do you have any final words before I send you and that bastard baby to hell?" she sneered. "This is not Richard's baby," Star whispered. "Stop lying! I followed him here the other night and stood in the window and watched him between your legs for hours." Hearing those words, Star knew at that moment there was nothing she could say that would make Richard's wife forgive her. Star closed her eyes and said a silent prayer, pleading for God to not punish her unborn child for her sins. The last thing Star remembered hearing was a loud crash, followed by several gun shots, right before everything went black.

****

Don made it halfway home before he reached for his cell phone to give Star a call. Something in his body told him the baby Star was carrying was indeed his child. After calling Star back to back several times and not getting an answer, Don began to worry. Making a quick U-turn in the middle of the street Don headed back in the direction of Star's house to make sure everything was okay. Walking up on the porch, Don grabbed for the gun he kept tucked in his waistband when he heard loud yelling coming from inside Star's house. Quietly leaning over the porch rail, Don peeped through the window and was shocked to see Star tied to a chair, bloody and bruised with an elderly woman standing in front of her, pointing a gun at her head. Don was confused as to what happened in just the little amount of time he had been gone. Don prayed the door was unlocked as he reached for the doorknob and slowly tried to turn it. His heart sank when the knob didn't twist. Realizing that he didn't have any time to waste, Don raised his foot and kicked the front door hard as he could. When the door flew off the hinges, Don rushed into the house just as two loud gunshots rang out. By the time he made it into the living room, Star was slumped over in the chair with blood pouring out of two large holes in the middle of her chest. Without hesitation Don emptied his entire clip into the woman standing over Star's body. Rushing over to Star, Don began untying her from the chair. Relieved that he felt a faint pulse, Don dialed 911 and begged for assistance. Within minutes he could hear sirens in the distance. "Stay with me baby," Don pleaded as he cradled Star in his arms. Paramedics and police swarmed Star's house asking a million questions. Don refused to leave Star's side as the paramedics began to do CPR on her. He held Star's hand as EMS placed her on the stretcher and whisked her outside to the waiting ambulance. Once they arrived at the hospital Don was instructed to wait in the waiting room while Star was rushed into emergency surgery. Don called King and informed him on what was going on. An hour later King and Mya arrived at the hospital with worried expressions on their faces. Mya sat in shock while she listened to Don explain to King everything that happened. Apparently, Richard's wife had been stalking Star for months. After following Richard to Star's house one day and seeing Star pregnant she automatically assumed the baby Star was carrying was Richard's and began to devise a plan to kill Star and the baby she was carrying. Mya was even more shocked to discover that Richard's wife was the same nice elderly clerk who worked at the courthouse and had given her and Ms. Brenda information on King when he was locked up. By the time Don finished filling King and Mya in on everything, a doctor walked into the waiting room and asked for the family of Star. They could tell by his body language he was about to deliver bad news. "We did everything we could to save Star but one of the bullets lodged in her heart. I'm sorry but we couldn't save her."

Epilogue

ONE YEAR LATER

Don and King sat under the large gazebo in the middle of King and Mya's backyard, sipping on cognac while they watched Mya push KJ and DJ on the huge, luxurious swing set King had installed. "I can't believe we are fathers," Don chuckled while taking a puff of his cigar. Although the doctors couldn't save Star's life, they were able to save the life of her unborn child. While Don, King, and Mya grieved over Star's death, they celebrated the birth of her son. Immediately following Star's death, Don filed for emergency custody of the child she gave birth to. Exactly one week after Star's death, Don and King sat nervously in the waiting room of the paternity clinic waiting on their names to be called. After the nurse swabbed the inside of Don, King, and baby DJ's mouth, she informed them they should have the results in the mail within a week. It was nothing they could do now but go home and anxiously wait. Since bringing him home from the hospital Don and baby DJ had formed a bond. Don would be devastated if it turned out he was not the father. When the large, white envelope arrived at his home a few days later from the paternity clinic, Don was so nervous he could hardly open the envelope. When he finally got the envelope open, his hands shook as he yanked out the papers and quickly scanned over them. A single tear slid down Don's cheek when his eyes landed on the bold red letters in the middle of the paper revealing he was 99.9 the father of baby DJ. The same day it was revealed Don was the biological father of Star's baby, King and Mya discovered Mya was pregnant. Apparently, King's wish of getting Mya pregnant had come true the week they locked themselves away in the honeymoon suite following the days King was released from jail. Enjoying the late-September cool breeze, the two men drifted off into their own thoughts thinking about how so much had happened in such a short amount of time. How had they gone from

King and Mya getting happily married just two years ago, to King and Don arrested and possibly spending the rest of their lives in jail, to burying Star? The only two good things that had come out of all their lies and deceit was the birth of their two beautiful children King Jr and Don Jr. "Daddy! Daddy!" DJ screamed as he ran up to Don with his chubby arms outstretched. Don's heart filled with love as he reached down and picked up his son. With Star's hazel green eyes and Don's caramel colored skin and deep dimples when he smiled, DJ was a spitting image of both his parents. "I'm about to take the boys in and put them down for a nap," Mya said, as she approached the gazebo with King Jr, who was the spitting image of his father with his rich chocolate skin and almond shaped eyes on her hip. Fatherhood made both King and Don realize it was time for a change. They decided now was a better time than ever to get out of the game permanently. They both had made enough money to live comfortably for the rest of their lives and with Richard being disbarred from practicing law after the videos of him and Star engaging in multiple sex acts while Star was underaged was submitted to the law ethics committee, King and Don no longer had to worry about their case being re-opened. As far as Mya and Don's little affair, well that would be a secret Mya and Don would take to their grave.

THE END

SCANDALOUS

Teri Woods Publishing
Presents
Family or Not, Some People
SCANDALOUS
Just Can't Be Trusted
A Novel
International Best Selling Author
Billie Dureyea Shell

"I think I am going to do it," Donesha said, suddenly sitting up on the therapist's couch—back straight and head up—she was so sure. "What is that...what will you do?" her therapist asked, waiting for Donesha to say the words they had worked toward for over a year. "I am finally going to tell my mom that...that I was molested." Donesha let out a full breath of air and slumped back onto the couch. "When she asks you by who...will you tell her?" She nodded yes, thinking back to that day at her grandmother's house. How she thought it was a game, just what kids did. Until she got older, years crept past and she felt different when he was around—a weird tingling in her stomach that made her feel angry. When she was thirteen, she'd put the pieces together but pushed the thoughts to the side. But now, after a year, she was able to say "molested" and her name in the same sentence. Now she was ready to say it out loud. "She'll probably know already that it was something at my granny's house." Donesha chuckled a bit at the thought. "I can't believe I'm here telling you all of this. I never dreamed that I would be able to talk this freely." It was an empowering moment, looking back over how far she had come since she put the jigsaw puzzle pieces of her memory back together. "Now remember what we talked about, right?" Ms. Palmer the therapist said. "However she reacts has…" "Nothing to do with me…it is from her own reality and perspective." "Exactly." Ms. Palmer was pleased, wishing that she could hug her client after all of the progress she had made. "Great. Our time is up. I'll see you in two weeks and you can tell me how everything went." They shook hands, an eager Donesha smiling from ear to ear, happy for someone to listen and be on her side. "Sounds good. See you then." Dr. Palmer watched as Donesha bounced from the room, through the lobby and out the door into the cold Chicago air. Leaving the small campus counseling center, Donesha smiled thinking about the winter break. Usually going back home meant a slew of emotions but today she was ready. "C'mon let's go." her twin yelled from the car. Hopping in the passenger side, the car eased away from the curb before she got her seat belt on. "I'm going to do it. I talked to her and I think I'm going to do it now," she said, just as sure now as she had been in the office. "Cool Sis...I'm with you. But do you think it matters?" The glare that Donesha shot at her sister could have killed a few dozen men. "Hell yeah, it matters. She was away at work when all that shit went on. You know how Grandma used to treat me." "I wasn't there all the time, remember. I don't know." "Ohhh yeah, that's right. You were off playing pianos and catching fireflies at music camps." Lanesha rolled her eyes at her sister's smart-ass comment and refocused her eyes back to the road. "Whatever, Nene...I didn't mean it like that. I'm just saying." "Yeah I'm just saying some shit to. I'm telling Mama—finally" They sat with quiet between them, just the sound of Lanesha's tires speeding up on the highway pavement. "So how are you going to say it?" Lanesha finally asked. "I got five hours till we get home to think about it." Home for the holidays brought the usual fakeness. Hugs, smiles, and promises that would never happen. But this year Donesha promised herself she was going to open her mouth and talk for once. It was hard finding the proper time. Once they got home, the girls were swept away on random shopping trips, store runs, and taste-testings. But on Christmas Eve, Donesha finally found a time to catch her mother alone. Late at night on the enclosed back porch, as her mother checked the mean smoker—Donesha went for it. Stepping out onto the porch sent her heart pounding like a drum. Yvette, her mother, barely looked up when she came out onto the porch. Her hair was wrapped up tight as a beehive while she shifted racks and checked the meat. "Ma...can I talk to you?" "Sure boo...you came out here to help?" She asked laughing. "Nah...not really. I just...I wanted to tell you about some stuff." She relayed the situation word for word like her therapist taught her—starting off slowly, with the time and specific situations so her mother would remember. "Remember when Lanesha got that piano camp scholarship and you were working out of town, and I had to stay by myself with Grandma?" "Yeah...I remember..." "Grandma...she wasn't that nice to me." Donesha thought about the nights being awakened from her bed to go rewash a cabinet full of clean dishes. Or being made to sit in the house all summer because someone called the house after eight p.m. "Oh girl...you know Mama is a damn firecracker." Yvette said not even bother to look her daughter's way as she swatted down her complaints. "I know that, but it wasn't about her being a firecracker. She was really bad to me and I don't want to be around her tomorrow." Slowly, Yvette's head crept up from the iron smoker. "You're not going with us?" "No…I don't want to go in her house ever again." "Why? What did she do that was so bad to you…" "She let me get molested." The words just fell out of her mouth. She didn't plan it, but there they were out in the open. "She what?" Donesha went over everything in as much detail as she could. "Mr. Clarkson…he was drunk." "Her boyfriend—Mr. Clarkson?" Donesha nodded, thinking hard on that night. The story had never changed for her, and the therapist had said as the years went on, the thoughts and memories of that night would get more and more vivid. "I screamed—I called for granny and she didn't come. The next day she told me not to tell anybody. Not even you." By now Donesha was bawling, her tears heavily streaming down her face in a flood. "Mama, I still think about it. I told myself it didn't happen but it did…it did." By now, a normal mother would have wrapped her arms around her daughter—and comforted her until the tears stopped—but not Yvette. Instead, she smoked a long Virginia Slim, gawking at her daughter as if she were some sort of alien. "Save all the crying shit, Donesha. You know you was fast girl." Yvette laughed taking a long drag of her cigarette and blowing it into Donesha's face. "Wha...what? He touched me...he made me do things...he told me not to tell." Donesha was baring her soul, something she rarely did—especially with her mother—but her words did nothing to penetrate Yvette's cold heart. "Your granny told me about your fast ass trying to fuck with Mr. Dennison's grandson. So don't tell me shit about that. You brought it on yourself." Donesha felt like dust, dirt on the floor, or even lower than that if it were possible. "No I didn't...I'm telling you what happened. After all this time…" She tried reasoning and giving valid rebuttals that she learned in therapy, but not even a year of therapy would prepare her for the reaction of Yvette Hollins. "Look baby, I'm sorry that happened to you, okay? But you got to remember to keep your legs closed and stay away from boys and men like that. You gotta be responsible. " In a few seconds ,Yvette was able to undo what had taken a year's worth of counseling to build. "Hell, it's up to you to hear what a man is thinking. If you were too slow to get out of there, then…" Yvette shrugged her shoulders, blowing cigarette smoke into her daughter's face. "Now what's really bothering you? Maybe it's the stress from school. But don't go on and on about that molesting shit, you hear me? Mama would have a fucking stroke if she heard you talk like that and…" Before Yvette could finish her sentence, a chime from the doorbell broke up their thoughts. "Shit, that's him. He's early." Yvette scrambled into the house toward the front door. Donesha walked behind her wiping her tears with her sleeve as her mother did what she did best, and that was ignore her needs. I hate this bitch, she told herself, as she followed behind Yvette. She eyed the knives on the kitchen counter. She envisioned herself taking the biggest one and jamming it into her mother's throat for not believing her. Then she would take the same knife, drive to her grandmother's, and do the same thing. Dumb bitches. Fuck them, she told herself as Yvette answered the door. "Hey Clarence. You're a little early aren't you?" She had never seen the man before. He was probably another entrant into her mother's revolving door of men. "Hey baby…" He came through the door hugging Yvette close but over her shoulder, his eyes were on Donehsa. She looked back for a moment, gazing at the hazel eyes of the man her mother was embracing. Then she noticed his arms, Donesha had a personal fetish with biceps and this creature had a perfect set, as well as pectoral muscles for her to press on. "Oh…Clarence…I'm sorry, this is my daughter," Yvette said, turning to introduce Clarence to her firstborn. But Clarence had already fondled her with his eyes, looking over every inch of the supple body of the twenty-year-old. "Nice to meet you," Donesha said, showing her teeth with an eager smile as she extended her hand to the new, handsome older friend of her mother. "The pleasure is all mine…" He kissed her hand like in the movies, planting a peck on her skin that sent chills through her body. "Alright…come on back here, I got us some wine," Yvette said, slamming the door and pulling her new man toward the kitchen. As Yvette talked and pulled, Clarence's eyes were still all over Donesha. She was used to it. Being so beautiful and developing early, always made Donesha a target for unwanted attention. But tonight she wasn't annoyed or eager to tell her mother like usual about unwanted advances. After the conversation tonight she was done telling her mother about anything. You don't want to listen to my words…So I'm gonna show your ass better than I can tell you, Donesha reasoned, as Clarence and Yvette disappeared into the kitchen. The talking and laughing continued, as corks popped and glasses clinked. "Psst…Psst…" Donesha swung around to see her sister in their bedroom doorway, waving her over. "Come here…" Slipping into their room, she lied down on the twin bed closest to the windows. Slumped in **exhaustion, Lanesha was ready to hear all the details.**

"What did she say?" Lonnie asked, wishing it was a different result than their mother's nonchalant demeanor. "She told me I was fast, and that Granny had told her a different story," Donesha said to herself, thinking of the old bitch that would say anything to cover up what happened on her watch. "Are you serious? She didn't believe you at all?" Lanesha asked. "Nope, but it's all good." "What does that mean...and who is Mama is laughing with in the kitchen?" Donesha wanted to tell her, but she was too busy plotting. If her mother didn't want to believe her and would much rather believe that she was, in her opinion, "A fast-ass little girl," then so be it, Donesha thought to herself. Let the games begin.

Chapter One

DONESHA

"Ashes to ashes and dust to dust. We now lay Sister Hollins to rest. A friend, a mother, and a grandmother..." And a bitch—the pastor forgot the most important characteristic of all. That bitch would never rest, the pastor had no idea that the woman we called our grandma was cursed. She was more like the devil, but you couldn't tell our mother that. She was boo-hooing, ready to fall in the hole and die with grandma. "Mama we are going to miss you." Yvette tossed in handfuls of dirt as they lowered granny's casket into the ground. It was embarrassing, seeing her cry and throw a fit over this rotten bitch. "Why is she doing all this?" I finally leaned over, asking my twin sister. She shrugged as my mother threw in a few roses, mixing with the dirt that would surely rot my grandmother's old, decrepit soul. "I mean… it is her mother. She's allowed to grieve, Nene…" So said my twin, but I didn't agree. Nobody should be allowed to grieve for that bitch. Looking at Lanesha was like looking in the mirror, except my hair was straight, with ombre-blonde tips past my shoulders. Today, my sister's hair was shorter and naturally curly. Our hair best described our personalities—totally opposite—and that was usually how we approached life. "Yeah, I guess. I'm not doing none of that shit though," I told her, as we continued to watch. She always saw stuff that I overlooked—like some calmer version of myself. "Look at all these people. Cousins that we have never met, aunts that have been away since we were young. Yet they all run back here…for what?" "Obligation?" "No…motherfuckers love negativity. They love this shit, and you know Mama loves putting on a show." "Yeah…just like her mama…" "May God burn her soul." "Agreed." We sat on those emotions for a second, thinking about the reasons we could be happy about someone's death, when Lanesha gave me another insight. "You know that's all a show. Mama has to keep up appearances." Lanesha was like my conscience, always reminding me about shit that I forgot. Like our mother was only about what people could see, everything else was pushed to the side and had been since we played with Barbie dolls. "Fuck that bitch," I hissed, and I knew my sister felt the same way. Our grandmother was dead and we couldn't bother to try and be sad about it. As the casket continued its descent, I had a flash of my childhood. I suddenly recalled the good times when my mother was around, and the bad times when we lived with my grandmother. It was torture, and I spent a lot of time hating this woman. Now she was dead, after all those years of praying she would finally be gone. I felt like rejoicing, screaming, doing a fucking cartwheel between the tombstones—but instead I stood in the lumpy grass of the cemetery, watching as people faked tears as they walked to their cars. "I just want shit to be real. Why is our family so fake...why?" It was more of a rhetorical question, because neither I nor my sister would ever have the answer to that. "Maybe because all this shit is fake. Everybody is cheating, fucking, and stealing from somebody else in this family, so why walk around and be real when you can't look in the fucking mirror." Her words stung me in more places than I cared to admit at the moment. I knew I was doing my fair share of dirt, but I always reverted to the loner side of myself—I had to do my dirt by my lonesome. "But we just know that she's gone now. That part of our lives is officially buried and we don't have to feel obligated to feel like her step-grandchildren anymore." It was some sad shit to say, but my sister always kept it real. "Yeah, you're right sis…" Lonnie's assessment was the most accurate way to describe the bitch that birthed our mother. Growing up, she treated us like step-children at the bottom of the barrel instead of like her own flesh and blood. "You know, a big part of me feels relief, like she got what was coming to her." I could only admit these true feelings to Lanesha. Anyone else would think I was some insane psychopath—but whatever. . "Naw, she got diabetes. What should have come to her was a bullet to the head." We laughed for a moment until Mama appeared before us. Her smeared makeup and bloodshot eyes made us straighten up like soldiers. "Girls, are you okay?" We didn't say a word, instead we looked at her like she was insane. I had enough. As the oldest, I was about to speak my mind right here in this cemetery. "Look around you…how many people do you see here?" Swiveling her head around, she joined us in taking a small survey. There were only about a dozen people at the cemetery, many of whom were running toward their cars before the pastor finished his words. "What does that have to do with anything?" Mama asked, annoyed at what already seemed like a moot point. "Everything. Nobody loved her but you. She was mean and evil to everybody else, and all these years…" "Girls, girls…let's get in the limousine. No need in having this conversation in front of everyone," Clarence said, on mama's side and defending her as usual. On the surface, he was the model husband coming to her rescue, but Mama didn't budge. Covering her hands with her ears, she took a stand. "No…I don't want to hear any of that right now." My Mama burst out into tears. "I've told you a million times I'm sorry…I'm so sorry…I can't go back in time and fix that stuff. What else do you want from me?" She tried hugging me but I wasn't interested in having her hands on me at all. "I'm so sorry for what happened to you and I promise I will spend the rest of my life making it right." She was preaching to the choir and saying all the stereotypical things, but I knew she didn't mean them. It was a rehearsed statement with no feeling behind it, that she'd built up from years of therapy. But in reality, there was no way you can apologize to a person for putting them in a place that facilitated rape. I hated to think about it. Actually it wasn't rape, it was molestation. I was a child too young to fight him off, and my mother wasn't there. My grandmother turned a blind eye and now here we are in a cemetery arguing over the woman who allowed me to be hurt. There was no way my mother could apologize for that, and here she was pleading for my forgiveness—but I was deaf to sympathy. I was more interested in revenge. It was the only thing that people understood. I've figured out over the years that it's a universal language. Everyone understands pain, and I wanted this woman in front of me who shared the same DNA running through my veins, to feel the pain that I felt. The pain of being left with an abusive grandmother and all the toxic people that ran in and out of her house, and all of the things we were subjected to. I wanted my mother to feel pain. "There is nothing you can do now. I just want to go home…I don't want to ride in the limo either. I'll just take an Uber or something." "An Uber…from the goddamn cemetery. Girl, are you out of your mind?" She was getting irritated and I loved it. Every time I was able to piss her off, I did, and there was no greater thing that upset her than failing to keep up a picture-perfect appearance. "No, Yvette, I'm not out of my fucking mind. We just put the psycho bitch that was your mother in the ground, and you're up here crying like Jesus died." I was ready to go to war and rumble right here in the cemetery, but somebody saved her ass. "Hold on wait…wait…" Clarence stepped between us. The way I was feeling I was ready to throw her ass in the ground with Granny. Two funerals in one day sounded appropriate to me, but like always, Clarence was here to put out the fire. "I'll take her in my car," suggested my mother's husband, the six-foot-two giant with biceps the size of a steroid-filled bodybuilder—the image belying the advertising executive that he was. "I have to go back to the office anyway." He said straightening his jacket, and was looking back and forth from me to Yvette. "Come on... people are watching. Don't let your emotions get the best of you." Yvette breathed fire. I knew on so many levels I had pissed her off but I was done holding my tongue about Granny. She was a mean bitch, and because of my mother Yvette, I spent a lot of time with that mean bitch. I wasn't going to pretend I was distraught that she was burning in Hell. Especially after the shit that went on in that house. "That's if you can be in the same car with me for fifteen minutes." I rolled my eyes at Clarence's statement. He always said assholic shit to me that got him either cursed out or completely ignored. As angry as my mother was at me, I ceased to exist when a man was involved. She no longer cared about our argument—she was now focused on her husband. "But we have people coming to the house." She pouted, damn near poking her lip out toward

Clarence like a toddler. "We talked about this, Yvette," Clarence said. This is why I drove my own car; I told you I have to wrap up this deal, then I'm all yours for the holidays. I can drop Donesha off on the way." I stood my ground, and watching my mother be disappointed about her husband not placating her with every move, made me do internal cartwheels. That's what you get bitch. Feel the fucking pain, it's nothing compared to what I feel. "Fine." She said, giving him a hug. Then she turned to me, trying to muster a smile. "I know you're angry and I'm sorry for all of that." She said it a million times, but I never believed her. She was just reciting some gibberish that sounded good. "You know...people will be asking about you." She had already moved on to what people were going to think if I wasn't at her mother's repass, but I wasn't budging. "I'd rather let Clarence take me home so I can lie down. Unless you want me to tell everyone the real stories about Granny and her house on Madison." She threw up her hands in disgust. I already knew that she wouldn't want me talking about being abused over the usual repass fixings. "Fine Donesha. Have it your way." She stormed off, walking with my sister trailing behind her to the limousine. Clarence and I watched as she smiled, shaking hands and hugging folks with politician-like precision. "I thought you wouldn't be able to pull it off." Clarence whispered as we turned and walked towards his car. "I'm not your wife, Clarence. I can do anything I want. I'm a fucking boss, not a peasant like her. That's why you want me, remember?" I whispered through gritted teeth. Walking through the uneven patches of grass in the cemetery, I felt invincible. My grandmother leaving the earth had shaken up my need for revenge. I was tired of holding in this pain, rethinking it every day of my life while my mother played the good mom and swept the shit I went through under the rug. Now walking beside me was her husband, her most prized possession, but she had no idea I had this man wrapped around my finger. "You make me so horny in that dress and the way you talk back to her. Whew… that shit makes my dick jump." He loved this shit and I knew it. He probably couldn't wait for a moment to step in and try to get me alone. I was wondering how he would do it and now he was pulling the car door open for me. "You couldn't wait could you?" I told him, seeing a sly smile part his lips. Glancing back at my mother, it was easy to see she was too busy smiling, hugging, and putting on a show to notice her man with his eyes on me. Lanesha was right beside her, kissing her ass—oblivious to it all. Meanwhile as always, my mama's men were infatuated with me, but this one was different. This time I wanted it, allowed it, encouraged it, and laughed about it. "Shhh, Mr. Jeffries. Your wife can still see us," I teased, easing into the car. "Not for long. Wait till I get your ass alone,." he said through clenched teeth as he slammed the door. He hopped in like a superhero going to fight crime and we were off, driving past my mother and sister as they hugged the family members and acted distraught. They waved and so did I, but I wanted to stick a special middle finger up at my mother as Clarence slid his hand up my thigh. "Oh, you look so fucking hot today." He was right. I wore a dress that was especially short because Granny would have deemed it to be disrespectful. Open-toe heels way too high for church and pink sparkle nail polish on my toes completed the look, because she would have thought whores wore that. I was saying "fuck you" to a few people today, my granny, and most of all my mom, by fucking her husband. It was my best magic trick of revenge yet; revenge was the only thing that kept me sane. "I missed you...you said you were coming by my apartment last night. I almost called Mom to see where you were." I laughed as we crept out of the cemetery, with my mother so engrossed in her grief and need to feel like a victim that she didn't even notice. "You could have—she wouldn't have suspected a thing," he said, turning out of the land of tombstones and fake tears. She didn't see that her husband was obsessed with me, that every time we were together, Clarence couldn't take his eyes off me. And who was I to tell him no; I am a grown woman of twenty-five years. He isn't my father, we have no blood relation so why can't I fuck him. I explained that to myself everyday like a prayer of my innocence for what I'm doing. But as a reminder that I was wrong, my phone rings. "Shit…" "Who is it?" Clarence asked, his hand still creeping up my dress to the edge of my panties. "Tron…" my boyfriend was calling and I was letting my mother's husband fondle up my thigh. "Answer it…" he ordered. "Put it on speaker…" I did as he said, while he peeled my panties to the side. "Hello." "Hey baby…you okay?" Clarence had found my creamy center and was now strumming my clit like a guitar. His fingers were soaked, moving ever so smoothly across the swollen nub of my clit as my boyfriend's voice filled the air. "I'm sorry again that I couldn't make it. I got called in at the last second and…" "I'm fine…everything's okay." I tried to keep my voice steady as my legs did an involuntary shake from Clarence's hand. "So, you sure you okay…?" "Yes…I'm fine…I'm okay baby. I just…I'm at a loss for words right now." I was out of breath like a sprinter but nothing working harder than Clarence's fingers. He played me, strummed me, stroking my pussy like he owned it all while merging onto the highway. I wasn't sure how to feel right now so I felt nothing...nothing but pleasure as I listened to my boyfriend and let my mother's husband's finger fuck me down the highway. All of this was a perfect combination, or a helluva storm. What could anyone expect, I was my granny's child, right? I loved drama, had an affinity for revenge, and I'm the queen at being vindictive. However bad my grandmother was, I am much worse. That's why she hated me, that's why she abused me and that's why my mother has to pay. May God burn my granny's soul.

Chapter Two

LANESHA

"I just don't understand your sister—why she couldn't play nice like everyone else." It had been a week since the funeral and my mom was still blabbing on about Donesha. It was always like this, I could have been the best daughter in the world but my mother would always bring up Donesha the problem child. "Mama. It's Thanksgiving; can we leave this alone?" "Exactly... here it is Thanksgiving and she's late. She really tries my damn patience." She complained about my sister being late, but here she was still cooking last minute add-ons to the menu. In a black cocktail dress and full makeup, my mother was peeling potatoes telling me about my sister being late. None of it made sense—in our family anything rarely did—but somehow I always had to play the peacemaker. "Ma...we didn't have the best relationship with grandma. I was away at school but Donesha was at home by herself for a lot of things, so she got the brunt of that" I tried to be nice as I could and explain it, but the shit that Granny did to my sister was unforgivable, so she can't blame Donnie for not wanting to be around. "I told you girls a million times that I didn't know it was that bad. I didn't find that out until much later. But besides all that, she's dead. We can't bring her back. All we can do is be respectful." She still wasn't hearing me. She wanted us to be respectful to someone that gave the utmost disrespect. "We can't let everybody see us fall apart." That was her problem, my mother was always so worried about appearances and what everyone else thought. "Mama you gotta understand we don't care what other people thought. It can't erase the things that…" but instead of listening, she covered her ears. "No, no, no, no...not today. I don't want to hear about any of that stuff today." This was her, my mother, the person that we couldn't talk to if it was about anything with real substance. She was all about the fake stuff and smoking mirrors. "Fine, Mama, fine...you never want to listen, you just want to keep shit in the past."

Before she could answer, the doorbell rang. "Oh...I gotta get the door. Hopefully that's your sister. Clarence..." "Yeah!" "People are showing up." "Okay, I'm at the door." I heard the the sounds of kids coming in, and a million hellos—then I saw him. Tron was in the middle of it all with his cocoa-brown skin and long locs, giving out hugs to my aunts, but I'm the one who wanted to be wrapped in his arms. "Oh, you're here." My sister was just a few feet in front of me, and I didn't even see her because I was so concentrated on him. "Hey!" We hugged, and I could already tell she was uneasy. "Where is Mom?" "In the kitchen. " "Good...I gotta put this food in the oven and..." A speeding toddler broke us up, running between us as the music seemed to get a few levels louder. Donesha pointed to the kitchen and I could already hear her and mom fussing. Moving toward the door, I got in the mix, giving hugs and getting cheek-kisses until I got to him. "Hey bro...what's going on?" I gave him a hug, innocent to everyone else—but to me it meant way more. My chest on his as we embraced and just close enough so I could hear, but the dozen or so people around us would have no clue. "Meet me in the garage in ten minutes," he whispered in my ear, and just as quickly as he hugged me, he let me go. But the way my heart was pounding, you would have thought he tongued me down. That's how much I loved Trontavius Pearson. The sound of my ass-clapping filled the garage. We always did it hard and fast when we were sneaking, but he was especially hard today. "It's yours, it's all yours," I told Tron, and it was the truth. The top of my head to the bottom of my pussy belonged to this man, but unfortunately all of him didn't belong to me. Still, I was like putty in his hands, or rather a quick fuck in the cold garage while my family gathered in the house for Thanksgiving dinner. But any time I had with him was stolen, so I took whatever I could get. "Yeah...toot that ass up." He lifted my dress more, grabbing onto my thong for leverage. As he pulled and I pushed, we made music with my pussy and his dick the main instrument. He was all I ever wanted and needed. We loved each other so much we couldn't keep our hands to ourselves. So at my mother's house on Thanksgiving we had no choice but to sneak away. Outside in the garage was the only place where we could be alone. Now with my dress up over my ass and my hands on my mother's car, he rammed me from behind. "Damn I missed you," he moaned as we moved together. He felt like sugar inside my pussy, a sweet treat that I couldn't get enough of. "I missed you too…" I squealed between pumps, moaning load as the wind blew snow and ice around outside. I didn't care that it was freezing. As long as Tron was with me, it was hot wherever we went. I waited for him to say he missed me too, or maybe even to tell me that he loved me, but I heard none of that. Instead he made an announcement: "I'm cumming…" and before I could make a sound, he pulled out of me and splattered his seed all over the garage floor. "What the fuck are you doing? My mom is going to see that." "Then clean it up." His dick was back in his boxers and zipped up before I could pull down my dress. Just like that, he had flipped a switch. He was back to being an asshole. "You're such an asshole. I didn't even cum. Why don't we come back later and finish." I wanted to hold him and feel close, but how romantic could we be in a dusty garage with the stench of oil and tires filling our noses? "I think we should stop this, said Tron." "What? Stop what?" "It's just beginning to be too much. I know we said this was just about sex, right? No feelings or nothing." I did say that. But of course that was before I fell in love with him. "Well we said we would tell each other when it was getting to be too much, and it's gotten to that point for me." I felt like someone dropkicked my heart, but I couldn't look bruised and hurt in front of him. "Okay cool." "So we're good?" Are we good? Hell no, we weren't good. I didn't even know what that question meant. "You can't make me cum at all...nothing. And you want this to be over?" Looking down at his phone, I saw Donesha's face. A picture of her on his home screen. When people did that, it meant only one thing. "So, you really love her?" "Come on man, with all of that. We said this wasn't permanent or nothing." I had fought with her my whole life, having to share everything I had with her. And now I was taking something of hers without her knowing, yet he wanted to ruin this small victory in my life. "So that's it Tron? What about everything you told me?" But he wasn't even looking at me—his face was in his phone. She was calling, her name lighting up his screen, and without hesitation, he answered. "Hey baby….Yeah I'm just getting some extra water. Here I come." Just like that I was invisible. He was too busy straightening his clothes and talking to her to even notice me. "Alright. I'll be right in." He was off the phone but his expression didn't soften. "So we're good...like this is our last hurrah right." He grabbed an old rag, throwing it on the ground where he spilled his seed. "You know what...I'm good anyway. Don't know why I even gave you a chance." We're cool. Right?" It wasn't the regular breakup. It wasn't like I could say I'll see you around. In the next five minutes I was going to be seeing him in my mother's house. Just be cool. Be cool.

He's testing you. He did that from time to time, told me that he was done fucking with me then on a late night I would get a text that he missed me and couldn't live without me. He hoisted the water on his shoulder and didn't even bother turning to look at me as he spoke. "Let me go out first," he said, not bothering to wait for me to answer. This, with cum stains drying on the garage floor, and my pussy wet and begging for more. This was the story of my life, getting left out in the cold, with no satisfaction from a man that I loved and happened to be sharing with my sister. I don't know how it started. We've been doing it so long it's hard to figure out at the exact point that I started fucking my Tron. It wasn't like I planned it, but now two years later here I am, sneaking back into the house after having my pussy filled in the garage. Except I felt even more empty than when I left the house. Tron said it was over, and now I felt numb; I didn't think him saying that was even possible. Back in the house it was business as usual—with aunts, uncles, cousins, and kids running about with no clue what I had just done. Music blaring, pots clanking, and enough talking that no one even noticed I was gone, except one person. "Where you been?" My sister was right there in my face, my twin. Looking at her was like staring in the mirror, except I looked way better. My hair was longer; she opted to chop hers off into a pixie cut that made her look like an alien. She was nothing like me—too vanilla—but somehow everyone loved her and I was the black sheep. "Just had to get something out of my car. Why?" She was all smiles, whispering like she was afraid someone would hear. "Come here...I need to talk to you." Sliding into the pantry off the kitchen, she started talking a mile a minute. "Slow down…" "Tron...I think...I think he's up to something." Hearing my man's name in her mouth raised my body temperature, but like everything in my life I shared it with my sister. "Really...like what?" I had to act surprised, nonchalant. "I don't know, he's been acting weird lately. Working a lot. I don't know, but I think he has a trip or something planned for me." A trip? The bitch didn't deserve a trip. I wanted to tell her the reason her man was missing was because he was in my bed every night he was at my place, but that would break her heart. Donesha wasn't hard like me. If she knew what was really going on, it would kill her—at least that's what Tron always told me. I can't tell her right now. When the time is right I'm going to leave her alone. Then we can be together. I've been dreaming of the fateful day for a year now. Watching and waiting for my turn to be happy, but now in this pantry I wanted to let the truth fly. I'm fucking your man, sis. He likes my pussy better than yours, get over it. I could taste the words like my mama's sweet potato pie, sweet in my mouth. I've wanted to tell her forever. Just one more month. He said he would tell her after Christmas. So instead of spilling the beans, I played along. "Oh, maybe he's just been working overtime." "You know, that's what I said. We're late on those bills too. Maybe that's it." She smiled. But I already knew why he was late on the bills. It wasn't easy taking care of my house and theirs too. "Alright y'all. Let's get ready to eat. Come on girls, grab a dish and bring it to the table." My mama peeked into the pantry, breaking up our time. "Mama, you rocking that red dress under that apron." She laughed, but it was the truth. My mother was the epitome of "black don't crack." "Thank ya, boo. Now come on. Let's get this dinner started." My Mom always did the holidays at our house, since it was the biggest. She would cook the whole meal and not break a sweat. Tonight she was even glowing, sashaying into the dining room were a few dozen people crowded around. "Alright, now let's bless this food. Clarence, you do the honors this year." My stepfather stepped up with his salt-and-pepper beard and chiseled fireman's arms. "Alright, everyone find your seat and bow your heads." I found a seat and of course Donesha had to sit across from me. Tron sitting right next to her, I tried to make eye contact with him, but he didn't even glance my way. It was as if I didn't exist when she was around. Maybe it's an act. Keeping up appearances, I told myself. "Alright, everyone bow your heads… Dear Lord…" I bowed my head but I wasn't praying. Instead, I slipped off my shoe, reaching my foot across the table and right into Tron's lap. "Dear Lord, we thank you for our family. Bring us together safely Lord." I was thankful for the big dick that my foot was rubbing across, the man that it belonged to, and that one day the man would be mine. But looking into Tron's face, he wasn't enjoying it. His deep frown and the pushing of my foot made too much commotion. A few eyes opened, and mine slammed shut as I pulled my leg back across from under the table. "Now let us all say…Amen." The room erupted into Amens as dishes were immediately passed down the table. The long table that seated twenty people, the kids' table behind us, and a few stragglers eating in the living room and kitchen made the house sound like a stadium. But I felt all alone. There was no one here by my side. I was sitting across the table from the man I loved, but no one could know that except us. Just tell them. Tell everybody you love me, I silently begged

Tron, wishing that he could hear my thoughts—but he didn't bother to look my way. Instead, he stood up and cleared his throat loudly. "Excuse me everyone. Can I have your attention please." It was like the earth stopped spinning when he spoke. I prayed he was going to do it, tell everyone he loved me right here at Thanksgiving. I sat up straight, smiling from ear to ear, but instead of Tron turning to me, he looked down to my sister. "Donesha, I love you with all of my heart. There is nothing that I wouldn't do for you and you are the best woman a man could have." When he smiled, his teeth were white as snow sparkling at everyone in the room. "Now tonight in front of everybody I want to tell them how much you mean to me." Rustling in his pocket, he reached for something, but he dropped to his knees so quick I could barely see what it was. "I love you, Donesha Hill. Will you marry me?" I couldn't have heard him right. I had to be dreaming, but while I was hyperventilating, my sister was screaming "yes" as the man I loved pushed a diamond ring onto her finger. The room was cheering, clapping, and screaming. Cameras flashed and everyone was happy. But not me. I watched them in shock as he hugged and kissed her. The tears streaming down her face were only matched by the tears coming down my own cheeks. The man that I wanted was marrying someone else—wait—not just someone else. He was marrying my sister and he did it right in front of my face. I wasn't sure, but this felt like war to me. Maybe he wants to see if you will fight for his love, I told myself, still in disbelief. "Can you believe it, your sister is going to get married," one of my aunts sitting next to me said, her face full of smiles and happy tears. I wanted to tell her "over my dead body" she would be getting married, but I didn't say a word. Instead, I smiled, a pretend fake smile stretched across my face as I planned my first attack—and that was telling her the truth.

Chapter Three

DONESHA

Tonight was a dream, something out of a movie. Driving home I couldn't stop staring at my new ring. Finally I was getting what I deserved. "Baby, you look at that thing anymore you are going to go blind," he told me, but I couldn't look away. "Look, this marks something new for us. No more games and lies. I'm going to be one hundred with you from now on." I tried to block the old Tron from my mind. The one that had me up crying all night mad and worried about the hoes that he was with. Now I had a ring on my finger, a new house, and a promise that he would be true. All I could do was accept him at his word. I smiled at him, tracing hearts in his hand, imaging the day we would be walking down the aisle. Months ago, I didn't even know if we would be able to be around each other, let alone getting married. "I really had no idea. This was a complete surprise." "You weren't supposed to. That's the way I planned it." This was a totally new Tron. Months ago he didn't plan shit but how to cheat on me. Now he was planning secret engagements. "Who knew...my mama...Lonnie...Who?" His face did this screwy frown when I said her name. "Your mom knew but Lanesha didn't know a thing." That wasn't a surprise. He hated my sister, couldn't stand her for some reason, and I knew the feeling was mutual on Lonnie's end. She didn't even say his name, she mostly called Tron "him" or some other pronoun, but never by name. "Come on...why do you hate my sister so much?" From the first time they met, Lanesha and Tron had been sworn enemies. She told me to leave his ass every chance she got, and tonight when he whipped out that ring she could barely tell me congratulations. "She's a hater. Did you see how she was looking at the table?" Rewinding back on the proposal, my emotions and thoughts were so high, I hadn't paid much attention to what my sister was doing. "She hugged me and said she was happy for me before we left." He sucked his teeth at that, pulling into the driveway. "I think she harbors some resentment toward you." This wasn't the first time he's said this and I still never understand what he's getting at. "What do you mean?" "You have a man, she doesn't. You and your mom fight, but that's because you are her favorite." I burst out in a deep laugh when he said that. "And...what does any of that mean?" "I'm just saying watch your sister. If she ever comes to you with some crazy shit, remember that we had this talk." He was always talking like this, telling me to watch Lonnie. "What about your mom. Does she know?" "Naw, I'll tell her one of these days." He said it like it wasn't a big deal. Like he went and bought new pants—not asked someone to be in his life. "One of these days?" "Baby, you know how Mom is... she's just..." "A bitch...a bitch is what she is." "That's my mom you're talking about." "Yeah, well she's a bitch. She never liked me and you probably didn't tell her you were proposing because she wouldn't approve." He took a deep breath, squeezing the wheel as he drove. I knew I touched a nerve but I didn't give a fuck. If he could talk about my sister, then I was going to tell him the truth about his bitter-ass mama. "I hope y'all can come together. We are going to be family." "That's the exact same way I feel about this issue you have with my sister." "That's different. Your sister is fucking evil." Lanesha was a spoiled-ass brat, but evil she wasn't. His mother's face was right beside "evil" in the dictionary, but I guess it's hard for him to notice it in someone that he shares blood with. "I think your reaching, Tron. I don't think my sister feels that way at all." He shook his head, pulling into our driveway. A brand-new, five-bedroom palace fit for a queen that I still wasn't used to yet, and now he popped me with another surprise. I guess when you get cheated on, this is the prize for staying. "Yeah whatever…you asked why I don't like her and that's my answer." Something about my sister always rubbed him the wrong way. I promised myself I was going to stay on some positive shit this year but I could tell he was pissed off. "And what about Clarence, ole dry ass? He barely wanted to shake my hand." That sent off alarms in my head. I had to change the subject. "Well baby, it is what it is. Let's not worry about everybody else. Your Mom, Clarence, my sister…let's just go inside and celebrate us." I waited for him to lower the garage door and turn off the car, but instead he sat there staring at his phone. "Come on…let's go inside." I was ready to thank him for this big-ass diamond ring, but I had a feeling I wasn't going to get the chance. "Naw, I gotta go to work, remember? Black Friday—I gotta be there early." "I wanted to lie in bed for a little while…show you how happy I am about my ring." I felt like a toddler begging for my man to come lie down with me. "I know, boo, but that ring doesn't pay for itself." That was it, I get a ring but I have to pay for it with the absence of the man who gave it to me. It was always like this—the house gets built, we move in, then he's gone for two weeks straight—to a training course. "I'm store manager now, and we're in busy season. Gotta be ready." "But at a car dealership? What do you have to do to get ready?" "You know we open at five, and I gotta make sure the guys move the new cars into the showroom." It was creeping close to two o'clock a.m., and as much as I wanted him to stay, I knew the drill. It was always like this; I was in a relationship and soon to be wife of a workaholic who would neglect me at any moment to go make a dollar. "Gotta pay for this house, your tuition...I got a lot of shit on my plate and I don't need you complaining about how much I work." I hated being dependent on someone, and him throwing my tuition payment into the equation was enough to make me vomit. "Okay, okay, I get it. You don't have to pile things on—I told you I would pay you back. This is supposed to be a happy night." Tron just laughed. "When you become a doctor, then we can talk about you paying me back. For now, somebody has to pay these bills." Just that quickly, my good night was turning into a nightmare. "Whatever, Tron...I'm not complaining. I'm just…" "Just what?" "Nothing...don't worry about it." I felt like taking the ring off and giving it back. I was happier when we were broke, before he got this job at the dealership. We were much happier back then. "Alright then." He didn't even bother to look up from his phone. I got out of the car slowly, waiting for him to say he loved me, but instead he backed out of the driveway before I was even in the house. I had a ring and no man, just this big house. Walking into the kitchen, I turned on lights, unwrapping my take-home plate from my mom's when I heard a knock on the door. "You forget something boo...?" I yelled as I walked to the door. I hoped for once that maybe he was just joking and staying home after all. Pulling open the door instead of Tron's locs and a sweater, I was greeted by a greying beard and a leather coat. "Clarence...what are you doing here? Where is Mom?" "She's at those sales. That shit y'all do every year...that wait-in-line stuff." I looked around in a panic. It wasn't a good idea for him to be here. "We need to talk…" "Clarence I don't think…" "Come on, I know he's gone. I saw him drive off." I didn't have an excuse; there was no lie I could tell. "Come on and let your pops inside. It's cold out here." I hated when he called himself that. He was far from my father. "Yeah, come in Clarence."

I corrected him. There was no need to call him pops or dad. He was my mother's husband and that was as far as the relation went. "So, congrats on the engagement." He half-laughed as he said it, his voice dripping in sarcasm like he was telling a joke. He peeled off his leather coat, and the tight shirt underneath showed every muscle on his body. "You shouldn't be here." I told him. "Why not? Why can't I come see and check on you." "Because...you know what that leads to." He didn't say a word. Instead, he went to the kitchen. "I'm going to get a glass of water. You want something?" I wanted him to go, but I simply shook my head no, following behind him a few feet away. "Dinner was good tonight. It was good seeing everyone." he walked around my kitchen like this was his house. Opening cabinets, getting water from the pitcher in the fridge, then leaning against the counter. "Yeah it was nice seeing everyone." I didn't mention my surprise; I knew that would only turn this conversation in a direction I didn't want it to go. "Yeah...and that ring. That's a big ring." He said, putting down his glass. "Can I see it?" He didn't wait for me to answer. Instead, he stepped closer, taking my hand. Just him touching me sent my heart fluttering and spinning a million miles a minute. "Damn...it's pretty." he said "I could have given you one bigger." "Clarence...I..."

before I could say another word, his lips were on mine. "Clarence…" "How you gonna marry him huh? You're supposed to be waiting for me." That was our plan. He would divorce Mama and we would run away together. But that was a plan five years overdue. I wasn't getting any younger, and sneaking around wasn't at the top of my list anymore. Pushing back out of his embrace, I stood my ground. "I can't wait for you forever. We had our time and it was wrong. I realize that now. I'm going to marry Tron and we will put all of this to bed." But instead, he pulled my left hand down to his zipper. His rock-hard dick was damn near exploding out of his pants. "Tell my dick that. Tell him that you are going to marry that punk and leave this dick...you know he's yours right? My dick belongs to you." I wanted to tell Clarence and his dick to leave but my body wouldn't let a sound come out. I missed him. I missed the way he touched and held me. It started out as revenge on my mama, but somehow my and Clarence's relationship translated into so much more. "Yeah...I already know you can't." The smile across his face was like he had me. He knew me too well. "I know he can't please you like I can." He was right about that, but I didn't want to tell him. It would have put lighter fluid on the already blazing ego that was Clarence Turner. "Clarence, we said we wouldn't do this anymore." I was begging like a child not to do this—not demanding—because I was powerless to him. And like every other time, he didn't listen and I was powerless to stop him. His lips on my neck came first, and then he was picking me up. My legs straddled around his waist as he held me up with ease and kissed me like I was the last woman on earth. "I love you...don't you know that? I love you..." He repeated it so much, I started to believe him. Over and over again he said the words as he sat me down on the marble counter top. Dropping to his knees I knew what was coming next—the spreading of my legs and my bare pussy right at his eye level. I felt his warm tongue parting my pussy lips, sending me straight to heaven with a diamond ring on my finger and a certified pussy monster between my legs. My eyes were rolling and calling out for God as Clarence did tongue maneuvers with my clit. I saw Heaven, zooming through clouds with mountains of orgasm hitting my pussy lips—when I heard the familiar mechanical voice. "FRONT DOOR," the alarm sounded, telling me that the front door had opened and so had the gates to hell.

Chapter Four

LANESHA

I was going to tell her the truth. My sister needed to know that I was fucking this man that was going to be her fiancé My blood began to boil thinking of Tron fucking her right in front of me, but when my eyes focused, I saw the salt-and-pepper beard dripping with my sister's pussy juices didn't belong to my man at all. "Clarence…. Donesha…?" I felt like I was about to throw up. Donesha always played the goody two-shoes and now I had caught her doing some shit that not even God would forgive. Donesha had her legs wide open, head back and eyes rolling and between her thighs was good ole Clarence. He looked like some pervert from a porno. "What are you doing here...how did you get in?" Donesha asked, scrambling to cover herself. "Where is Mama?" I thought about telling her she was right behind me. "The key you gave me, remember?...we're going shopping—you told me to come over..." Clarence couldn't even look at me. He scrambled to his feet, wiping his face as Donesha jumped down from the counter. "Where is your mother?" "She's at the fucking store waiting on us." I told him. "Please don't tell your mother." He had the audacity to ask me that with my sisters pussy still fresh on his breath. "That's all you have to say to me is 'don't tell Mom'?" I couldn't believe what I was seeing, but after the shit I've done, on second thought I could. All the times I've fucked Tron at a family gathering just because it felt fun to be that dangerous. I played with fire and for some reason I always thought my sister was too much of a goody two-shoes...not anymore. "With Clarence...really, Donesha." I wished I had a gun on me. I would have shot him right through his frosted beard for playing my mama, but a part of me could see why. Clarence was fine as fuck. "I'm sorry...I..." His weak ass started stuttering like some retarded fool. "Please...it was a mistake." "A mistake. So you just fell head-first into my sister's pussy?" Both of them looked to the floor. This was the bitch he wanted to marry. Tron skipped over me and was going to marry this bitch. "I always knew you liked her more than me." I laughed at all the Christmases he gave her an extra special gift, and now I knew why. "How long has this been going on?" "Sis...I can explain." Donesha finally said something, but I wasn't trying to hear it. Phone-in-hand, I pulled it up and they both jumped like they had seen a ghost. "I said...HOW LONG HAS THIS BEEN GOING ON? Tell me that, or tell it to Mom." Clarence bucked up, taking a step toward me, and I took two steps backwards. "Look. Your mom doesn't have to know." he kept walking forward, his belt buckle jingling with his every step as I backed up toward the door. "Clarence...what the hell are you doing?" Donesha screamed after him, but his eyes were trained on me. "Get the fuck away from my sister." I could hear her opening a drawer and getting a knife but I had something way better than that. "She's going to tell, and Yvette doesn't need to know about this." Reaching into my purse, I pulled out my Beretta, flicking it off safety. "Don't take another step toward me motherfucker, or I'm going to blow your brains out." I meant every word, until I saw him move. It was instinct, my finger sliding to the trigger and pulling. It happened so quick that I couldn't move until I heard screams ………

About The Author

New York Times & International Best Selling Author Billie Dureyea Shell was born in Compton California and now lives in Ladera Heights with his wife and kids who he loves to spend time with. He is the Owner of several properties in the Los Angeles area and gives back to his community by providing low income housing to those who need it. He stated "It doesn't matter where you at or where you from it's what you do with your time. There's nothing you can't do if you put your mind to it".